EXPOSED

ELIZABETH MEYETTE

BORIS PUBLISHING

EXPOSED

BY

Elizabeth Meyette

BORIS PUBLISHING

Published by Boris Publishing

BORIS PUBLISHING

Cover Design by Meyette Photography

❀ Created with Vellum

To Franklin & Evelyn and Annie & Clarence, who gave me life and unconditional love.

ACKNOWLEDGMENTS

A book is never written by just one person. The input and insights of many go into developing a good story. My deepest gratitude to my beloved husband Rich, who creates my cover art, acts as webmaster, and designs my marketing materials. He is my main supporter, cheering me on when I despair and listening to my ideas during our "staff meetings," which often include adult beverages.

As usual, my books are a family affair since my children also support me in so many ways. Thanks to my daughter, Kate Bode, who took me to a sporting goods store and patiently gave me lessons in fly fishing and tying flies. To my son, Matt Hanley, who helped me with the ideal cribbage hand for Layla. Cribbage games between Matt and Rich are epic. To my daughter, Kristin Hanley, who gives me superb marketing ideas.

In addition to family, friends and colleagues help to create a successful novel. Thanks to my Write-in group, Patricia Kiyono, Annie O'Rourke, Diana Lloyd, and Tracy Keely, who have lived this book with me since its inception in 2016. Their patient listening and encouragement helped me shape the story I believed in. Thanks to my dear friend Kim Keith, who helped me with medical terminology and patient care information.

Again, my appreciation and love to my beta readers, H.J. Smith, Luana Russell, Sarah Yoder, Tina Jacobs, Anne Stone, and Monique Carter for their honest and helpful critique of my drafts of *Exposed*. Without their input, neither my story nor my characters would be as strong. Thanks to my editor, Julie Sturgeon, who takes what I have written and raises it to a new level with her guidance and suggestions.

Thanks to you, my readers, who travel the story with my characters. You bring life to them, and I hope they bring life to you.

ONE

Monday, May 4

He stared at the grainy newspaper photo taped to the mirror. His fingers gripped the black marker so tightly that his fingernails dug into his palm. He didn't notice. His vision tunneled to the photo. Yanking the top off the marker, he leaned over the dresser, his arm poised.

A movement caught his attention.

On the street below, early risers gripped cups of steaming coffee from the local cafe as they hustled toward their day. Look at the guy exiting the drugstore. What if he got so tired of being pushed down that he shot the place up? The woman getting out of her car, digging through her huge purse. What if she were looking for a gun? What if the little guys of the world rose up and said, "We're done with this shit?"

Maybe the only way to swing that system around was to take action.

He stood taller. "We all can take our part and make it happen. I plan to start one bitch at a time."

He was sick and tired of people who had it all. People who

didn't give a crap about what happened to the other guy. Damn her.

He pressed the marker against the photo, the black ink bleeding into the newsprint. As he drew, his lips pulled back against his teeth in a half smile, half grimace. He drew a circle, then another, and again, until a bull's-eye covered the woman's face.

***

"MORNING, MISS FORRESTER."

Layla smiled at Jimmy Hunter, who stood at the entrance to her office. "Hey, Jimmy. How are the Tigers doing today?"

Jimmy's stocky figure, typical of someone with Down syndrome, hurried through the door, his steps short but determined. He always wore a grin that lifted her spirits, and the sparkle in his brown eyes hinted at a mischievous side. His dedication to the Detroit Tigers was admirable—and infectious. He even had her following the team's record.

"They're trailing the Orioles, but they'll come back. Don't you worry, Miss Forrester." He straightened his ubiquitous bow tie and pressed his hands down his clean white dress shirt—a proper exclamation point.

"I'm not worried as long as you're watching out for them." She winked at him.

He waved his hand. "Aw, Miss Forrester. You're so nice."

Setting the mail on the corner of the desk, he beamed at her. "Right where you like it! High five, Miss Forrester." He held up his hand and Layla slapped it.

"High five, Jimmy. You made my day."

His cheeks flushed. "Oh, you always say that."

"Because I always mean it."

"Have a good day, Ms. Forrester." As he left, Jimmy waved, his smile wide.

"You, too. See ya', Jimmy."

"See ya'," Jimmy said over his shoulder.

It was their daily ritual, a ritual Layla looked forward to. She liked rituals because she liked to know expectations.

"Got a minute?" Mariana Rodriguez leaned against the door-jamb, her dark eyes twinkling. She cocked a thumb in Jimmy's direction. "He's awesome. Glad you got him this job."

She had joined the firm just a few months earlier but had already put her stamp on the place. While she stood only five foot two, she owned a room when she entered it, charming all present with her gregarious personality. Mariana could engage Layla in a long conversation, and Layla wouldn't mind.

Mariana was the only person in the firm Layla considered even close to being a friend—not that they hung out. But Mariana wasn't afraid of her.

Layla nodded. "Hiring Jimmy was one of the best decisions I've ever made."

She brushed back a wayward strand of hair. Initially, guilt might have been her motivation for hiring him. She'd prosecuted Jimmy's brother, Trevor, and he'd been convicted of a felony for dealing drugs.

As messed up as Trevor was, she'd seen his affection for Jimmy, and with him incarcerated, the only person caring for Jimmy—that would be using the term loosely—was their abusive father, who had a couple of convictions under his belt, too.

Mariana pushed off the doorframe and strolled into the office. "It was a win-win. His life is better for sure. Thank God Mr. Hunter was willing to let you find a group home for Jimmy while his brother is in jail."

She nodded again. "Keeps him away from dear old dad."

"Hey, want to do lunch today?" Mariana tilted her head in question, her thick, black hair cascading over her shoulder.

Layla stiffened. She liked Mariana, but she didn't fraternize with anyone at the office. She worked through lunch so she could leave as early as possible.

Mariana picked up on her posture and took a step back. "No problem, *amiga*. Another time maybe."

Layla tapped the stack of mail Jimmy had deposited on her desk. "I just have so much work to do."

"Sure." She hesitated at the door. "You know, friends are the carbonation of life."

"What?" Layla stopped tapping.

"Friends, also love, bring sparkle, effervescence to life." She smiled and left.

Layla rubbed her forehead. She could have accepted her invitation. It would only have been an hour. But she avoided friendships at work. *You avoid friendships period.*

A throbbing behind her eyes told her coffee was overdue. A nice, steaming cup would make going through the mail a little more bearable. Getting to the coffee machine in the break room would not be as friendly as Jimmy and Marina had been. Among the staff she was known as the Ice Queen. She clenched her jaw, straightened her shoulders, and grabbed her coffee mug.

The sound of her Jimmy Choo heels on the tile floor was comforting.

Click. Click. Click.

Bitch. Bitch. Bitch.

Layla could almost hear their thoughts as she passed each paralegal's desk in the main office area. Walking the gauntlet, she called it. She avoided meeting their gazes.

Who cares? Only one thing matters.

It didn't matter that all the paralegals rolled their eyes behind her back as she passed or, mentally if not actually, flipped her off after they greeted her with a cheery "Good morning, Ms. Forrester." It didn't matter that Seth Thomas scowled at her through the door of his cramped office. The tiny office that— according to him—should be hers. She glanced his way in time to catch him glower at her before looking away.

Why would any parent name their child after a timepiece? "Seth Thomas" was engraved on the face of the clock in her living room. For a while, she'd been tempted to throw her crystal vase at it. But the clock had been Mom's and the vase Grandma Jane's, so it continued to reside on the wall, and gradually lost its effect on her blood pressure.

Go ahead, Seth Thomas, make faces at me if you want.

Just the smell of freshly made coffee eased the tightness in her jaw. After filling her mug, she added hazelnut creamer. She took a deep breath, savoring the aroma of roasted beans mingled with the nutty sweetness. With a sigh, she took a long sip, then straightened her shoulders for the trip back to her office.

It didn't matter that her secretary, Angela VanDenberg, flashed a pasted-on smile and handed Layla a stack of papers and messages as she entered her large, corner office. The office Seth believed was rightfully his. The office twice the size of his, with windows looking out on Monroe Avenue.

It didn't matter that her boss, Roland Gage, had insisted she take this office. Roland insisted on a lot of things, and soon, Roland would insist she sleep with him.

None of these things mattered.

Entering her office, she relaxed just a tad, having survived the daily gauntlet of their resentment, hatred and ... well, fear. The fluorescent-light buzz assured her that, indeed, another day at the office had begun. She placed her coffee cup on her mahogany desk, paused at the window, and considered the view of downtown Grand Rapids.

The trees surrounding Rosa Parks Circle flaunted their clusters of white blossoms, and pedestrians had doffed their winter coats for light jackets, some even in shirtsleeves. Nowhere was spring more beautiful than Michigan.

Catching her reflection in the glass, she smoothed a recalcitrant strand of chestnut-brown hair back into place before she sat down in the burgundy, Italian leather chair that cupped her body like a glove. Working in a law firm offered luxuries she hadn't had as a prosecuting attorney, including a salary that allowed Dad to live at Brookside.

And that was all that mattered.

Eyeing her desk, she tapped the stack of envelopes Jimmy had brought.

"Might as well get to it."

The framed picture beside the mail caught her eye. Her parents smiled at her from the deck of a ship on the last trip they had taken together twenty years earlier. Layla caressed the frame, tracing the outline of her mother's, then her father's face. Now that Mom was gone, only one thing mattered. Dad.

The ringing phone jarred her from her reverie. A gruff demand came through before she even had a chance to say hello.

"Did you get those case files I left for you?" Seth's question— no, accusation—grated on her nerves. Not only did he have a curious name, he always sounded like he needed to clear his throat. Layla cleared hers.

"Good morning, Seth. I haven't gone through everything on my desk yet." She remained cool, direct.

"Well, I'd sure as hell appreciate it if you would follow up on them. I know I'm not as important as you ..."

Layla hung up the phone. *Screw you, Seth. Get over yourself. I got this position because I was the best qualified.*

Why didn't he just come down the hall and hand the damn files to her if it was so damned urgent? But then she'd have to interact with him, and they had interacted enough. What had she found attractive about the always rumpled, athletic-body-gone-to-flab man? He was older than she by almost ten years and passing forty had depressed him. Well, three years ago she'd passed thirty, so she got it, and forty was on its way. That was one expectation she could count on.

She grabbed the stack of mail. Most of the interoffice mail came in large manila envelopes with spaces for the addressee that could be crossed off and reused. She picked up one that was new, only one name listed on it—hers. Inside was a regular white business envelope. She tugged it out and frowned at the scrawled writing on the front.

"Ms. Layla Forrester, Bitch."

Oh crap. Another day at the office.

She thought about tossing it into the trash but reconsidered. Pulling her engraved letter opener from the nook where it rested in its place in the middle drawer, she sighed and slit the envelope flap.

A haze of powder drifted toward her face. Instinctively, she held her breath and turned her head. Her blood turned icy. Stunned, she sat in silence trying to comprehend what had just happened.

"Ms. Forrester, I have those ..." Angela stopped in the doorway. "Are you all right?"

"Get out—" Layla shouted.

A look of pure loathing crossed her secretary's face.

"—and call 911!"

Angela spied the powder. Her eyes widened. As her hands flew to her mouth, the folder she carried dropped, sending papers shooting out to the floor. "Oh my God!"

TWO

Above the rapid-fire tattoo of her heart, Layla heard the far-off sirens. Sweat pricked her scalp and beaded on her upper lip as she sat motionless waiting for the first responders. *What is that? Anthrax? Sarin? Will I end up in ICU, attached to machines?* She saw the image of her body, white as marble, on a medical examiner's table.

Hunkered into the corner of the couch farthest from her desk and the opened envelope, she tried to protect her shallow breathing through the scarf she held against her nose and mouth. The light scent of Chanel did nothing to comfort her.

Who sent it and why?

Line up the suspects. I'm sure there are hundreds.

Inside the office, an eerie silence surrounded her. So different from the chaotic noise when all employees had been instructed to leave the main area. Chairs had tipped as people leapt from them, some women had been weeping, some people, praying. At least, she'd heard a lot of "Oh, my Gods." Praying or cursing?

Now, she was alone. Granted, she preferred to be alone most of the time, closing her door to the office gossip and drama.

But she had never felt this alone in her life.

Mom had once told her, "Friends are the dessert of life, Layla. Fill your plate with them. And true love, that's the icing on the cake."

Her gaze traveled to the picture of her parents on her desk. A Mediterranean cruise. The sapphire-blue sea was a cruel backdrop to her mother's pale face and sunken eyes, signs of the cancer that was already destroying her once healthy, vibrant body. Beside her, Clarence Forrester did not look at the sea or the sites, but only at Margaret, his eyes shining with adoration. His robust complexion a stark contrast to her pallor. He had an arm around her shoulders as if to shield her from what they all knew was ahead—more chemotherapy, more radiation, hospice, and death.

Layla swallowed. *I'm not ready to see you yet, Mom. Dad still needs me.*

She jumped as her door opened and something from a 1950s-sci-fi movie entered. A tall figure shrouded in a lime-green hazmat suit peered at her through a helmet that looked like an inverted tumbler plunked on his head. After closing the door, he strode toward her as best he could. Slowly raising his arms, he reached out to her. She shrank away; it was the childhood terror of watching sci-fi movies on Saturday afternoon, her head tucked into Dad's chest. She whimpered, and shame coursed through her veins.

His face was hidden behind the visor that reflected her own appearance back to her. At first, she didn't recognize her face—it was a mask of helplessness, her brows drawn together, her eyes bright with terror, her lips pressed together. Every emotion she had fought to hide from others was now exposed on her face.

She loathed this man who saw her vulnerability. She loathed this man she could not see.

JACK TRENTON HAD SCANNED the room as he entered, noting the envelope and letter opener on the desk sprinkled with white powder. Looking around, he spotted a woman hunched on the couch, arms crossed, as if trying to stay warm. Dropping the scarf that muffled her face, she sat up straighter, her lips pulled taut, and blinked.

She didn't fit the description he'd heard from the staff members in the outer hall as he'd suited up: snob, tyrant, cold. But he did see something in her eyes. Defiance? Anger? He supposed he would be angry, too, if someone had done this to him. Though he wanted to, he couldn't continue to study her, or he'd lose track of his task.

"I need you to remain where you are while I scan the room and they assemble the decontamination tent." He sounded robotic, scratchy through the respirator he wore. He wished it sounded more reassuring.

She merely nodded. She was a cool one.

He took out the hazardous materials scanner and circled her desk. He froze as the screen indicated a hazardous substance—anthrax? Sarin? Fentanyl? While it was a low level, probably mixed in with another powdery substance, it had to be treated with full decon procedures. He sent the data back to central control.

The woman now sat ramrod straight. She had covered her nose and mouth with her scarf again, but her gaze was steely, unwavering.

"What did you find?" Her words sounded muffled through the scarf.

Trying to fool her would be useless. Obviously, if she had the ability to be in this much control in a situation that had often caused burly men to weep, sugarcoating wouldn't work this time.

"Traces of a toxin. You will need to go through a complete decon ... decontamination procedure."

She nodded her head once. Up, then down. No indecision, just acceptance. That was good. He'd thought she might argue. Might insist that she knew what was best for herself.

She jumped at the sound of three loud knocks on the office door.

Maybe not as cool as she wants to appear.

"We're ready with the decon tent." Another raspy, mechanical comment.

Jack looked at the woman. "Ms. Forrester"—someone from the office had spoken her name as if they had a dirty sock shoved in their mouth— "can you stand?"

"Of course," she said through the silk fabric. She stood, looking him in the eye.

She was almost as tall as he, slender and graceful. Her posture was straight, her shoulders back, head held high. Bold.

This is where she gets belligerent.

He opened the door to the outer office, indicating a blue tent with a shower head attached and a large, square blue pool surrounding it.

"You will need to disrobe, put all your clothing, jewelry, shoes, in this large plastic bag. Then shower using the soap provided. You'll need to wash your hair, too. There's a robe provided for you when you're finished." He wished he didn't sound so other-worldly.

"Do you have slippers to wear so I can drive home?"

Her husky voice called to mind a bar he liked where the whisky was as smooth as the jazz. He could listen to her talk all day. He stared at her for a minute, glad he was wearing this bulky suit.

She eyed him. "Slippers?"

"No, no slippers."

"How am I supposed to drive? Barefoot?"

"You aren't driving. You are being transported to Mercy Hospital for observation."

"What? I can't go to the hospital ..."

Here we go.

Another man in a hazmat suit took her arm, leading her to the tent. She whipped her head back at Jack, brown eyes blazing.

"I can't be taken to the hospital. Can't you do something? I didn't touch the powder ..."

The tent flap closed, muting her silken voice.

Jack stood looking at the tent. He wanted to see more of this woman...literally and figuratively.

THREE

"Is there anything else you can tell us, Miss Forrester?"

Layla stared at the detective. He was clearly annoyed with her. No surprise there. She'd had no information for him. Wasn't it bad enough to be stuck in this hospital bed? Now she had to endure the inquisition. For which she had no answers. And the IV attached to her left arm was the instrument of torture. She tried to cross her arms but winced when the IV stopped her.

He snapped his notebook shut.

"Look, Detective Smith ..."

"Smythe. Rhymes with writhe." He pushed up steel-framed glasses that matched his steel gray hair.

"Sorry. Detective Smythe," she emphasized the pronunciation, "as I told you, I am not well liked by the people I work with, but I can't think of any one of them who would want to hurt me."

"Maybe kill you." His reply was as cold as the ice it sent through her veins.

"Or that." She rubbed her arms.

"Fine. If you think of anything that may help us find this

person, don't hesitate to call. After all, we are trying to help keep you alive." He dripped sarcasm.

She leveled her gaze at him, and he blinked. "If I knew something, don't you think I'd tell you? You're the one with all the evidence—the powder, the envelope. Test it for prints."

He handed her a card then rose. Towering over her, he reminded her of John Wayne. She expected him to hitch up his belt and mosey on out. "Feel free to call anytime, Ms. Forrester." His mouth twitched, but he bit back whatever retort he'd planned to leave her with.

Drained, she leaned back against her pillows. What did he expect her to do? Make things up? People might consider her an ice queen, but she was an honest ice queen.

Glancing at the clock, she was shocked to see the time. She was usually at Dad's by now. She had to get out of here.

She picked at the tape covering the IV needle in her arm. God, she hated needles ... and hospitals, and doctors, and illness, and weakness. Sitting up, she wiggled the needle, then swooned, her stomach lurching. It had taken some doing when they'd inserted the needle for the IV. Since Mercy Hospital was attached to a medical school, medical students and interns got to experiment on patients—she had been an unfortunate one, drawing a timid young man who apparently also hated needles. He tried five times before he gave up on the back of her hands and finally inserted it in her arm. She still hurt from his efforts.

Yanking this out was a final decision. She was not going to go through that again.

Just as she was about to rip off the tape, someone entered.

"And what do you think you're doing, Ms. Forrester?" His baritone voice held a mix of concern and amusement.

She turned quickly, pinching the crook of her arm as she did so, sending more pain shooting from the needle.

"Ow!" She hadn't meant to squeal. Which doctor was he, and how much was he going to probe and poke her?

Stepping to the bed, he gently pushed her back against the pillows.

"Trying to sneak out early? Before you get the full round of treatment?" His eyes danced as he checked the IV.

Studying him, Layla thought she should reassess her dislike of doctors. He was tall—close to six feet—with almost black hair and arresting china-blue eyes that made her forget her despair for a moment. His blue oxford shirt, the color of a cloudless summer sky, intensified the effect of his eyes. Surely, he wore tinted contacts.

And he should at least wear the requisite white lab coat to protect people from this seductive effect.

Despite his busy patient schedule, he must have found time to work out because his frame was muscular and solid. He smiled at her, and she experienced a rush of pleasure, and for the first time in the last several years, an unfamiliar yearning tingled within. She actually cared if he liked her.

"And what misery are you going to put me through?" she asked.

He chuckled. "No misery. Just checking up on you. Where were you planning to go?"

"I need to go visit my father." She sounded small and weak. Breathing deeply, she regained her composure. Even Dr. Good-Looking wasn't going to see her get emotional. "I visit him every day after work. If I don't show up, he'll worry and think something's wrong."

He gazed around the room at the monitors attached to her.

"Looks to me like something is wrong," he said. "Someone threatened your life today. Do you have any idea who would do this to you?" His eyes held hers, and she wanted him to come closer.

She scoffed. "Line them up. I'm not in danger of winning a popularity contest." She kept interactions business-like. Friends got close and then they deserted you. She didn't go out for drinks after work with colleagues, she didn't attend the Christmas party or baby showers or weddings. When people got close, she got hurt.

The only exception to her business-only policy had been the brief fling with Seth which, in retrospect, she still didn't understand. Perhaps it was because he'd been safe. She hadn't loved him and probably never would, so if he'd left, it wouldn't have hurt.

But who had she offended enough to threaten her life? A chill snaked along her spine.

"Well, you've been through quite an ordeal today. Perhaps your father could come visit you this time."

She shook her head. "No, you don't understand. Dad lives in an assisted living facility. He has multiple sclerosis, and I'm his only family." She fought the urge to yank out the IV again even in front of this doctor.

"Which nursing home? Can you call and talk to him? Explain what happened?"

"No!" she snapped, then held up her hand. "Sorry. My cell phone is in my purse back at my office. They wouldn't let me bring it today. And this antique"—she gestured to the phone on the bedside table—"doesn't work. Besides, I don't know his number by heart, I just say, 'Call Dad.'

"I don't want him to worry. I don't want him to know." She twisted the sheet around her fingers. "It could...kill him...if he hears about this." She glanced at the blank TV screen. "Oh, no. Was it on the news?"

She picked at the IV again.

He stilled her hand with his. His touch was warm, gentle, and she gritted her teeth against the pleasure it brought.

"Layla."

His soothing tone washed over her. She closed her eyes, resisting his charm.

"Look at me." He placed his finger beneath her chin and raised her face to his. He'd leaned down, his face near hers, the sandalwood scent of his aftershave wafting to her.

She gripped the blanket.

He smiled. "Where is your father? I'll go to him, explain what happened. If he needs medical attention as a result, I'll be there as will others on staff." He placed his hand on hers. "I'll tell him gently, I promise. He needs to know. He may know already and need reassurance that you're okay." He pulled out his cell phone. "Here, I'll take a picture of you. Smile and wave. Let your father know you're all right."

Despite the red flags his beguiling presence triggered, she softened. Maybe he was right. There was no way she was getting out of here tonight, and his idea made sense. She sat up, lifted her hair and then shook her head to let it fall around her shoulders. "I probably look a mess."

He raised his eyes from his phone to meet hers. "You look beautiful."

His blue eyes took her breath away.

She glanced at the window.

"I know. I'll take a video. You can tell him yourself that you're fine." He stopped adjusting the phone settings and gazed at her as she adjusted her thin hospital gown. He cleared his throat. "Okay, Miss Forrester, take one."

Feeling self-conscious, she couldn't speak at first.

He stopped the video. "Need to write a script? I don't think I can hold cue cards and videotape you at the same time."

"No. It's just ... I've never been videotaped before."

"Oh, c'mon. Don't you and your girlfriends take selfies all the time?"

She looked away. She had no girlfriends. She went to work. She visited Dad. She went home. She had only Dad. And she had to reassure him that she was all right, even though she didn't know yet if she was. She sat up and shook her loose hair again.

"All right, I'm ready. Let's get this over with."

"That's the spirit. I promise it will hurt less than yanking out your IV would have." His laughter embraced her, and she smiled.

"Okay, get ready for take two." He sat on the bed beside her. "I'm starting in three...two...one. Go!"

None of the many presentations she'd given to groups had ever felt this awkward. She straightened her gown and smiled into the phone. "Hi, Dad." She waved her free arm. "There was an incident at the office today, and as a precaution I'm in the hospital overnight for observation. I'm fine, so don't worry. Love you." Her words caught. She took a deep breath. "I'll see you tomorrow." She blew a kiss.

Leaning back against the pillows, she swallowed the lump in her throat. She needed a minute, so she closed her eyes. Then, peering out of one, she glanced at him. "How was that?"

"Perfect. I'll go there right now and show him. So, where am I going?" He poised his fingers above his phone ready to type in the address.

"His name is Clarence Forrester. He's at Brookside Independent Living, 800 Morton Street, right off Fulton."

His eyebrows shot up. "Really? That's right in my neighborhood," he said, typing in the address. "I pass right by it." Finished typing, he put his phone in his shirt pocket.

"I can't thank you enough—" She stopped. "I don't even know your name."

"Jack. Jack Trenton."

FOUR

Jack's visit with Layla was all he could think about as he navigated rush-hour traffic. That husky, whisky-smooth voice. The thin cotton gown she'd worn. He'd had to concentrate hard on keeping the conversation light. She'd assigned him a task, and he took it as willingly as a dog fetched a stick.

Her father's nursing home was less than a quarter mile from his place. He must be quite a guy for his daughter to be that dedicated. If she visited him every day after work, she must have a limited social life.

Her social life is none of my concern.

He planned to drop by, show her father the video, reassure him, and leave. He'd be home to a microwave dinner in no time. And a beer. He needed a beer after his encounter with Ms. Forrester. Layla. Yeah. Layla.

"You got me on my knees, Layla," he sang.

Brookside Assisted Living was on a quiet side street in a gentrified older part of town. The newer building with sleek windows and concrete construction contrasted with the early twentieth-century brick homes and apartment buildings it was tucked in among. This was a high-end facility; the monthly cost definitely beyond his pay grade.

He pushed through the outside entry but was stopped at the next door. He pressed the bell. A young college student with a thatch of light brown hair, a scruffy beard, and earrings that looked the size of a penny stretching out his earlobes buzzed him through. He greeted Jack at the reception desk.

"Good evening. Can I help you?"

"Yes, I'm Jack Trenton, and I'm here to see Clarence Forrester."

The kid spun his chair around and reached for a clipboard. The white lab coat he wore gave him a more professional look, and his clear, intelligent eyes belied his dorm-rumpled looks.

"Great, I was just going to check on Clarence. Just sign the visitor log and I'll take you to him."

Jack followed the kid down the hallway, noting that the exterior doors had safety locks, just as the front one did. This facility didn't want any of its patients wandering away and getting lost.

They stopped outside room 105 and the kid knocked gently. "Clarence? It's me, and you've got a visitor."

He pushed the door open to a cheery studio apartment decorated with prints of trout arcing out of streams, and anglers' rods arcing to land them. A vase of fresh flowers stood on the center of a small table, and another vase on the bedside table held a lucky bamboo.

In a recliner sat a pleasant-looking man who resembled the man on the Monopoly board with white hair fringing his bald head, though no moustache. He held a newspaper folded to the crossword puzzle and greeted them with a broad smile that faded when he spotted Jack. He looked past him.

"Where's Layla?" A furrow creased his brow as he attempted to get up. Obviously, he hadn't seen the local evening news.

The kid placed a hand on his shoulder. "I'm sure she'll be

here soon. But this guy, Jack Trenton, is here to see you right now."

Clarence's gaze shifted from the kid to Jack, suspiciously. His eyes were bright; he definitely knew something was up. Clarence glanced at the clock beside his bed. "Layla is usually here by now. Just tell me." He drilled Jack with a look of determination tempered with hidden fear.

Jack stepped toward the chair, holding up his hands. "Layla is fine." Her name stuck in his throat, as if speaking it somehow made her his. He cleared his throat. "Your daughter had an accident—rather, an incident at work today."

"What happened? How is Layla?" He sat forward, his hands gripping the arms of his chair.

Jack took a deep breath that puffed out his cheeks, then exhaled.

"Someone sent her a letter that contained a white powder."

"My God!" He struggled to rise. "Was it that Thomas guy?" Clarence glowered at him. "What did he do to my baby?"

Jack frowned. "Thomas who?"

"That bully with a clock name."

The kid gently pushed him back down on the chair. "Take it easy." He spoke softly but with authority. Clarence glared at him.

"Layla," Her name stuck in Jack's throat again as the image of her, lifting her hair and shaking it free, struck his brain like a lightning bolt. "Your daughter is being held for observation overnight at Mercy Hospital. My initial on-site analysis indicated a low-level toxin mixed with a white powder, perhaps talcum powder. It's in for tox screening right now so they'll know better how to treat it."

"You a doctor?"

"No, I'm on the hazmat team. I was a first responder today."

Clarence nodded appreciatively, his eyes never leaving Jack's. "You were with her. You took care of her."

Jack shifted from foot to foot. Warmth spread through him. He shook his head to stem the damn warm fuzzies. "Yes, I was there."

"And she's all right? Is she sick?"

"I stopped by to check on her, and she seemed fine. In fact, she was trying to pull out her IV to escape to come and see you."

Light filled Clarence's eyes and a proud smile lit up his face. "That's my girl. Feisty as hell." His chuckle rumbled from deep within. "So, she sent you to assure me, right?"

"Well, I offered ..."

"Sure, you did." He studied Jack. "You'd better look out, son. She's bossy as hell, too." He indicated the chair opposite his, and Jack sat down.

A grin spread across Jack's face. "That she is, sir. I taped a message from her for you." He pulled out his phone and scrolled to the video. He handed it to Clarence.

When the video ended, Clarence studied him, a knowing gleam in his eye. Then his smile faded, and his face darkened. "Who would do this to my little girl?" He stared at the floor, his hands hanging limply over the arms of his recliner.

His pathos caught Jack off guard. He coughed.

"There will be a full investigation, sir."

Clarence's gaze snapped to him. "People get the wrong impression of her. Think she's cold, uncaring." He looked around his place, speaking softer now. "No one knows just how caring she is."

"Yes, sir."

"Police don't know who did it?"

"Not as far as I know."

"Probably that damn Thomas guy. Never met him, but she told me about him. I warned her about him. Jerk." He stared at the floor as he spoke, then looked at Jack. "She's stubborn though." He reached out and touched Jack's knee. "Is she going to be all right, son?"

Jack jerked back in his chair. No one, not even his own father, had ever addressed him that way. His old man might have said something to the effect of, "How the hell did I ever have such a screw-up for a son." But never just, "son."

The kid, who'd been leaning against the counter in the tiny kitchen area all this time, held up his hand. Jack had forgotten he was even there. "You need to get some rest. This news got you all shook up." The kid attempted a fair Elvis impression and wrote something on the chart.

"I was agitated, just a little wound up for a minute there. We're just going to visit for a bit, Doc." He winked at Jack.

Jack twisted in his seat and looked up at the kid ... who wasn't a kid, now that he looked closer. "You're a doctor?" He couldn't hide his surprise.

The kid gave him a half smile. "Yeah, dude. A regular Doogie Howser." He scratched his scruffy beard. "Later the guys and me, we're going out ding-dong ditching."

"I'm just so ..."

"No worries, man. Happens all the time." He looked at Clarence. "Half an hour, then Grandpa here," he nodded at Jack, "has to go."

Clarence chuckled again. "Got it, Doc." He turned to Jack, serious now. "Tell me everything. Everything you know."

Sitting forward in the chair, Jack described what protocol he'd followed in Layla's office, the hazmat procedures she went through, and his visit to her hospital room.

Clarence relaxed back into his chair, then squinted at him. "That was mighty nice of you. To stop and see her."

"Well, I was concerned about her." Jack looked down at his hands, loosely folded and hanging between his knees. *Admit it, Trenton, you wanted to see her and hear her speak again.*

"Mm- hmm." Clarence rubbed his jaw. "You know, Layla is tough as nails, but someone tried to hurt her. Since you're concerned about her, I'm going to ask for a favor." He patted the wheelchair beside his recliner. "I'm pretty much stuck here, so I can't watch out for her." He leaned forward, the humor gone from his eyes. "You cared enough to check on her tonight. Please, however you can manage it, watch out for her."

Jack's smile faded. *Watch out for her? How the hell am I supposed to do that?* But the plea in the man's eyes gave his heart a funny twitch.

Clarence reached for his arm. "Please, son."

There it was again. Son. He smiled. It sounded nice; he wished he'd heard it more.

"I'll do what I can, sir."

"Promise me."

"I promise."

Their eyes locked for a moment, the air electric with favor asked and promise given.

Clarence leaned back and broke the spell. "Want a beer?"

"No, I have to head home." Jack gazed at the collection of mounted fishing flies in a shadow box on the wall. "Those are beauts." He stood to examine the collection closer. "I like this Blue Wing Olive." He studied the tiny, delicate strands of hairs tied around the hook. The musky smell of a river came to mind, and he almost drooled.

"Yup, tied it myself. I did all of those. There's an Elk Hair Caddis and a Hex Spinner. How do you like this Royal Coachman?"

Jack turned to him and smiled. "Mr. Forrester, we have a lot to talk about."

FIVE

Tuesday, May 5

Layla eyed the IV in her arm, damning the tether that held her captive in the hospital bed. She'd endured a night of being awakened to take vital signs, people talking in the corridor, and loudspeaker pages unsuccessfully muted for the night. And for the brief time she was able to sleep, a dream haunted her, of white powder chasing her along the gauntlet that became a dizzying maze of desks. No matter where she turned, the powder followed. She wore a blue paper gown, flapping open in the back, and paper slippers. People were pointing at her and laughing. She'd awakened with a start, heart racing, sweat soaking her gown.

She stared at the ceiling. Who was laughing at her the hardest? Whoever sent her that letter was a coward hiding behind a threat. But had it been just a threat?

Finally drifting off, she struggled through another dream. Again, her face was reflected in the hazmat guy's visor. She might as well have stood naked before him. The thing she'd been able to hide from others, block from others, was screaming at her from his visor: I am vulnerable.

If she ever saw him again, she'd rip off that damn mask and tell him to go to hell right to his face. What face? That was the hardest part. This nameless, faceless man had witnessed something in her that no one else ever saw.

She tugged at the IV. *I'm fine. Surely, they'll discharge me today.* What were they waiting for? A doctor with his retinue of first-year med students had come in at six that morning to examine her. Not the hot doctor who had checked on her the previous night, unfortunately. Maybe she wasn't interested in dating, but she never minded looking.

This morning's doctor said they were still waiting for some final tests to come in, but so far, she exhibited no symptoms of any kind. She blew out a long breath and picked at her blanket. *Come on. Come on. I have work to do.*

As if hearing her command, the door opened and a short, plump blonde woman in a crisp lab coat hurried in pushing a mobile computer cart. The stethoscope around her neck would reach mid-breast on most, but it dangled almost to her waist. Her cheery smile amped up Layla's already impatient mood.

"Good morning." She actually sang it.

Good Lord, get me out of here. Layla tried to keep her face impassive but felt her brow furrow with a loud *Hurry up!*

"Oh, I see we've awakened on the wrong side of the bed this morning. Well, maybe my news will cheer you up." Her clear green eyes twinkled, and Layla tightened her right fist. "I'm Dr. Kozinski. I've been looking at the test results. There was a small amount of fentanyl found, but mostly it was just ordinary powder. Calcium citrate."

"Calcium citrate?" So it was just a threat. He—or she—was a coward.

"Yes. A supplement available online or at your local health

store. You didn't aspirate any fentanyl, and all your tests came back fine." She patted Layla's fist. "Looks like you can go home today."

Layla's shoulders relaxed and she smiled. "That's great news." She threw back the blanket.

"Hold your horses, darlin'. Not quite yet." Dr. Kozinski logged onto the computer and scanned her records. "We'll need to take a final round of vitals, we have a prescription for you at the pharmacy, and you have discharge instructions and papers to sign." She winked as if they shared a secret. "It'll be a while." She eyed the IV bottle and the line tethering Layla to the bed. "I think we'll leave that in for a while longer. Wouldn't want you to disappear on us." She winked again and toddled out.

So, Dr. Hottie had ratted on her. He must have written something in her chart about finding her trying to escape last night. *Loss of hot points for you, Doctor.*

She flopped back on her pillows and hissed another sigh. She wanted to get back to work. That case she was reviewing would be in court before long, and she had to be ready. She checked the clock. Nine a.m. Surely, she'd be out of here in time for lunch with Dad.

RUSH HOUR TRAFFIC snarled up the lanes on US 131 and cars crawled along in funeral procession lethargy. Layla was surprised they'd discharged her; certainly her blood pressure had been sky-high by the time they came in with the paperwork. Apparently, the discharge process was designed to keep patients longer, since the snail's pace with which it transpired had taken all day. She had just been released at 4:30 p.m.

That added another grand to my hospital bill.

Her stop at the hospital pharmacy had taken almost forty-five minutes because she arrived just after another patient who needed nine different meds. She'd forgotten to ask why she was there in the first place. She didn't need an antibiotic, so what medicine had been prescribed for her? When she finally held it in her hand, she was livid. Sleeping pills. What the hell? She tried to give it back, but the incredibly patient pharmacist explained that once the prescription was handed over to the patient, it could not be returned. Layla was certain smoke was coming out of the top of her head as he smiled at her and then slid his gaze to the next person in line.

She'd had to call a taxi to take her back to the office to retrieve her purse and car. The office was empty by the time she arrived, but a custodian let her in. As she stood in front of her desk, an eerie wave of bewilderment flowed through her. Every trace of powder was gone, as if nothing unusual had happened. Her laptop and phone were slightly misplaced, the only confirmation of the previous day's threat. Shaking off the disorientation, she snatched her purse, phone, and keys and left. She was already late getting to Dad's.

The trip to the office had been slow enough, but now she was back in snarled traffic again.

She turned the audio system to smooth jazz to relax her jangled nerves. All she wanted was to sit with Dad, maybe play some cribbage.

Just feel safe again.

SIX

Jack relaxed back into the chair, one ankle resting on his other knee. He'd decided to visit Clarence again after work and talk more fly fishing. It certainly wasn't because Layla visited Clarence daily, though maybe he'd see her again.

He balanced a can of soda on the arm of his chair and smiled at Clarence. "So, you tied all these flies yourself? They're great." A photo album was propped against his crossed leg. He thumbed through the pages of photos of tied flies, of Clarence grinning as he held up a large trout or poised with his rod arced back, the line curving gracefully.

Jack turned the page and sucked in his breath. Smiling directly at him was Layla, proudly holding up an enormous trout. Her deep-set brown eyes flashed joy and delight. The sun was shining, casting red highlights through her thick, wavy brown hair, her smile wide with pleasure.

"You okay, son?"

Jack let out the breath he'd been holding. Quickly turning the page—though he wanted nothing more than to stare at Layla's face—he shifted in his seat. When he looked up, Clarence's eyes twinkled at him, his mouth hitched up in a half smile.

"She has that effect."

"Oh, I was looking at the fish." Jack closed the album and handed it back.

"And you get *Playboy* to read the articles."

Jack felt heat climb up his neck. "I don't get *Playboy*." This was nuts. Women didn't affect him like this.

"Glad to hear it."

They burst out laughing just as the door opened. With his back to it, Jack couldn't see if it was Dr. Doogie or one of the aides that came to check on Clarence.

"Hey, Dad,"

His heart skipped a beat at the honey-mellow sound.

Jack wanted to spin around and see her face, but he forced himself to turn slowly, then smile up at Layla.

"Dr. Hot ...Doctor, what are you doing here?"

He looked for Dr. Doogie but must have missed him.

Clarence grinned at his daughter and held out his arms. "Are you okay, Sliver?"

She leaned in for his hug and kissed his cheek.

As they hugged, Clarence squeezed his eyes closed, but not before Jack noted the concern in his eyes despite his welcoming smile.

She straightened. "I'm fine." She sat beside him.

"Jack told me everything that happened."

She nodded her thanks, then took Clarence's hand. "The little bit of fentanyl wasn't enough to hurt me since I didn't inhale it."

Clarence kept hold of her hand, his eyes bright with happiness. Jack could only guess what strength it took to hide his fear from her. And what about her? Here she was, strong, unafraid. Or was she?

"Tell me about it," Clarence gave her an encouraging smile.

She opened her mouth, hesitated, and raised her eyebrows at Jack.

"Jack here came to visit me again today, Sliver. Isn't that nice?"

Jack nodded in agreement, but he didn't like Clarence's sly grin.

"Yes." She drew the word out. "Yes, I suppose it is."

She described opening the letter, releasing the powder. "I moved away from it before I breathed it in or it touched me. They thought it best for me to be checked out at the hospital, so I went, and they kept me overnight for observation." She nodded to Jack. "Thank you for being kind enough to visit Dad and reassure him that I was fine. They just discharged me a while ago. Traffic was a nightmare, and it took me almost an hour to get here."

Jack noticed she hadn't said a word about him arriving with the hazmat team. In fact, she made it sound like she went to the hospital on her own. Was she trying to downplay the danger so Clarence wouldn't worry? They played a game of "I'm not afraid, so you shouldn't be either."

"According to Jack, you tried to discharge yourself last night." Clarence chuckled. "My feisty girl."

She turned on Jack. "Yes, and I have a bone to pick with you." Now her eyes blazed, lighting up the golden flecks. He was mesmerized. "You wrote something in my chart, didn't you? Saying that I tried to pull out my IV and leave."

She pointed a finger at him, the mauve tip moving closer to his chest. He wanted to grab that hand and pull all of her closer to his chest.

"Because of you, they wouldn't take the IV out until I'd signed the discharge papers and been released." She glowered at him. "I hate IVs, Dr. Trenton."

"But I'm not—"

She waved him off. "I surely did not appreciate that."

He held up his hand to explain her mistake in thinking he was a doctor, but an aide entered.

"Time for dinner, Mr. Forrester." The aide halted at the sight of Layla. Her dull eyes narrowed. "Oh."

One syllable, thick with disdain. She tossed back her stringy, light brown hair and sniffed.

"What's on the menu tonight, Crystal?" Clarence set the photo album on the table beside him.

"Corned beef and cabbage." She glared at Layla.

"My favorite! But this place will be tootin' all night." His eyes crinkled up as he laughed until he started coughing. "Thanks, Crystal."

"Welcome." One last glower at Layla and she left, shutting the door behind her.

Clarence clucked. "She still blames you for her brother Dwayne getting fired."

"Too bad. He brought you the wrong medication, Dad. You could have—" She crossed her arms.

"You caught it, Sliver. I'm fine."

"Dwayne was pretty angry with me." Layla stared at the door, her brow creased.

"I'd invite you to join me, but I have to put in a reservation for dinner guests by noon." Clarence looked from one to the other. "But you two could have dinner together. There's a nice little bistro just down the road. Called that, too, something bistro. What was the name? Oh yeah, Fulton Street Bistro. Good food, nice atmosphere."

"I need to get home ..."

"I'm sure she has plans ..."

Their excuses toppled over one another.

"No, I think, after the trauma of the last two days, a nice

dinner out would be good for Layla. Just what the doctor ordered." He chuckled.

Jack rubbed the back of his neck. Geez, he would like nothing more than to sit across the table looking into deep brown eyes flecked with gold. Eyes he couldn't look into now for fear of exposing his attraction.

"Dad," Layla scolded as she drew out his name.

Her face was a rosy color that made her look so damned beautiful.

He'd planned to watch a little of the Detroit Red Wings game and call it an early night because tomorrow he started work at 6 a.m. But instead, well, tonight he could take some time to look into brown eyes that turned up at the corners when she smiled.

"Sounds good to me." He looked at Layla. "We both have to eat. Why not?"

Why not, was right. Because she might just smile that smile and he'd be toast. Because low restaurant lighting might just make her eyes sparkle. Because when she spoke, it was a siren song.

She shrugged. "All right, Doctor."

"I'm not—"

Clarence interrupted him. "You kids get on your way."

Jack shot Clarence a look, but he just grinned back. Layla rose and grabbed her purse. She leaned down to give her father a kiss and hugged him, not letting go until she kissed his cheek again.

"See you tomorrow, Daddy.

Daddy. She sure didn't sound like the cold, harsh woman her staff had described. No, unlike them, he wouldn't describe her as an ice queen.

SEVEN

The "little bistro" Dad had recommended was an upscale restaurant where atmosphere consisted of candles flickering on the tables, carefully positioned décor, potted plants, and wall hangings that muted dinner guests' chats, creating a hushed, even romantic, ambiance.

I wonder how he even knows about this place.

Layla wished he had suggested a chain restaurant with standard posters of movie stars or sports teams—maybe some big-screen TVs with a different sport playing on each one or a pub where the home team scored and all the diners whooped and cheered, interrupting any kind of deep discussion.

Fulton Street Bistro drew patrons in and wrapped them in a cocoon of intimacy at their table. With soft jazz playing and space between tables, other diners would not be privy to conversations. A little too much atmosphere, which could result in a little too much exposure.

The hostess assigned them to a waiter dressed in a crisp white dress shirt, creased black trousers, and shiny black shoes—no polo shirt, khakis, and tennis shoes here. She'd have a talk with Dad tomorrow. She lifted her chin and followed the waiter to their table, avoiding any curious gaze that might identify her as that woman who'd received deadly mail. She'd seen a clip on the news last night and had been furious they'd played it up so. For ratings, she was sure.

After the waiter handed her the menu, she studied it. For a long time. Despite the fact that she had barely eaten the hospital lunch of mystery meat and wilted—not intentionally—salad, her appetite had deserted her.

What were these curious twinges coursing through her body as she sat across from Dr. Hottie? He'd lost points for ratting her out for trying to escape last night, plus, he'd sat there chatting with her father like they were best buds. Why did that bother her? He'd actually been very kind to Dad.

"Thanks again for visiting Dad and reassuring him that I am okay."

"No problem. He actually lives quite close to my place, so it wasn't inconvenient at all. And he's quite a guy. I enjoyed talking fly fishing with him."

"Yes, I take him all the time." *Oh, that sounded territorial. And you haven't taken him very often lately.*

The waiter returned for their drink order. She ordered a manhattan. Somehow, ordering a beer didn't seem appropriate at Dad's "little bistro." Jack must have concurred—he ordered a scotch.

After they ordered drinks, she studied the menu again. Dr. Trenton had set his down, ready to order, but she continued to stare at the words on the menu, making no sense of them.

Steady, girl, you do not need a complication like this man in your life. You're on track and progressing according to plan. Stay strong and end this here.

Sighing, she put the menu down and looked around at the

other diners. That way, she avoided his deep sea-blue gaze. A dangerous gaze. A tempting gaze.

"You're lost in thought."

His baritone timbre triggered that curious tingling again. She tried to think of anything but how attractive he looked in the candlelight.

"I'm wondering how Dad knew about this place. I mean, is he sneaking out to dinner with some pretty ladies from Brookside Assisted Living? I can see them rolling along Fulton Street in wheelchairs, white hair flying in the breeze."

His laugh was contagious, and she couldn't help but join him. She didn't laugh much. Hell, she didn't laugh at all. He'd made her laugh two days in a row. Their gazes held as their laughter quieted, and she looked away.

Back off, Layla. Warning signs are flying all around you. Keep it cool. "So, Dr. Trenton—"

"Jack? Jack Trenton?" A petite blonde in a blue knit dress that hugged her figure stopped at the table.

Jack rose slowly, dropping his white linen napkin on the table. "Meredith. Hello."

Meredith's bright periwinkle eyes slid from him and burned through Layla.

"Layla, this is Meredith McKenzie. We work together."

Meredith shifted her gaze to Jack. She arched one brow.

Layla suspected she was waiting for him to add what else they did together, startled at the twist of jealousy that grabbed her around the heart. She held out her hand. "Nice to meet you, Meredith."

But Meredith's gaze still rested on Jack, whose gaze slid back to Layla.

"Yes, we *work* very well together. I hope we're on the same *shift* again soon, Jack." She gazed down at Layla's outstretched hand, dismissing it. "Nice to meet you, too, Linda."

Layla pressed her napkin to her lips, muting a chuckle. She was used to being treated coldly, but this woman didn't even know her and already disliked her. *Therefore, it's not about me this time.*

"Are you also a doctor?" Layla asked, trying not to bait the woman by adding *on the night shift?*

Meredith frowned at her as if she were a bug on the chair. She looked at Jack. "Doctor?" One corner of her mouth curled up as her gaze caught Jack's. "Nice line." She sashayed away with the intentional gait of a woman who knew a man was watching.

And Jack watched.

And it ticked Layla off. *What difference does it make to me if they play doctor?* She didn't want complications in her life, and this man had all the earmarks of complications.

"Sorry about that. Meredith is a bit ..." He dropped into his seat. "She's—"

"Beautiful," Layla finished flatly.

He glanced in the direction Meredith had disappeared. "Beauty is only skin deep."

It was Layla's turn to raise an eyebrow at him.

He studied the menu. "What are you thinking?"

Layla stared in the direction of the lingering musky perfume. "I'm thinking she must have been a cheerleader with all that perky energy."

His mouth quirked to the left. "I'm thinking the ribeye."

"What?"

"The ribeye. I meant, what are you thinking of for dinner?" Leaning on the table, he wiped one eye and the laugh he'd tried to suppress slipped out.

Her face flamed. She'd looked like a fool thinking he'd wanted to know her thoughts. Her temper flared. "You set me up."

His head jerked back. "No, I didn't. What do you mean?"

"You asked an ambiguous question, then suggested I answered it wrong."

His eyebrows shot up. "No, I didn't. I asked a question and you gave me a thoughtful answer. An answer that made me laugh because you're so witty."

She eyed him suspiciously.

"Lighten up, Layla. We shared a laugh, not at your expense, at the reward of getting to know each other." He covered her hand with his.

She wanted to pull away. Yet there was her hand, still beneath his, his warmth seeping into her skin, his hand just resting lightly, no pressure, just reassurance. Why wasn't she pulling away? Why was she putting up with this?

She yanked her hand away. "Easy for you to say."

"Have you decided?" The waiter placed their drinks before them. She hadn't even seen him approach. He looked expectantly at Jack, waiting for him to order for both of them.

"I'll have the pork medallions," Layla said. Or perhaps shouted by the look of the nearby diners who threw curious stares her way. She'd be damned if some man was going to speak for her.

Jack smiled, quickly erased it, and ordered the steak and a bottle of cabernet sauvignon.

She raised an eyebrow at him. "A bottle of wine? Are you planning to linger tonight?"

One side of his mouth hitched up. "We're getting on so well, I thought we should make an evening of it." He raised his drink to her. She stared at him for a few seconds, then reluctantly raised hers. He clinked his against it. "To laughter."

She fought a smile. He obviously hadn't intentionally baited her.

He swished the ice in his drink a few times. "Does your mother live in this neighborhood, too?"

"My mother is dead."

"I'm sorry." He took her hand, and she savored the warmth. She savored it too much.

Pulling away, she wrapped both hands around her drink.

"Tell me about her."

Frowning, she eyed him. Was he serious? His gaze held hers, his smile soft. She didn't talk about Mom. But he was listening, waiting.

"She died of breast cancer when I was thirteen." She smiled. "Mom was a fighter, and she lived longer than they'd predicted." She cleared her throat.

But the tenderness in his blue eyes, soft in the candlelight said, *Go on. I want to hear more.*

"I was just starting my...to mature, and she wasn't there. I had my first real crush, dealt with mean girls at school, and navigated my teens without her. Dad did everything he could, but it's not the same, you know?" She wiped at the moisture on her glass. "All the things you need a mom for, buying a prom dress, your first heartbreak, planning your wedding..."

He sat back and his eyes narrowed.

What did I say?

He glanced at her left hand, and his eyes softened. He sat forward again. "Tell me something you loved about her."

Did he really want to hear this? What didn't she love about Mom?

Smiling, Layla cast her mind back and grinned. "Every Saturday morning, we had to clean the house. She'd crank up moldy oldies like Journey and Eric Clapton, and we'd wrap our hair in bandanas and dust, sweep, scrub. When we were finished, we'd go out for ice cream, even in a snowstorm." Avoiding his eyes, she studied the diners across from them. "Well, enough about that."

"Layla, I didn't mean to upset you. I honestly wanted to hear about your mother. Am I forgiven?"

"Nothing to forgive if you're being honest with me."

He winced. "About being honest with you. Layla, I'm not—" He leaned forward, almost bumping the arm of the waiter who had appeared from nowhere.

"Your soup, madam." The waiter bent to serve her, one eye on Jack. He turned to the tray stand beside him and carefully lifted another bowl of soup, setting it cautiously in front of Jack.

"Will there be anything else?" The waiter looked at Layla this time, stepping back from the table.

"No, that will be all," they chimed in unison, but Jack's several decibels louder.

Layla stared at him. He'd been so calm and gentle all this time. Where was this fire coming from?

"A little hard on that waiter, weren't you?" She leveled her gaze at him.

Jack rubbed the back of his neck and massaged along his right shoulder. Did he wince?

"I've just been trying to tell you something, and I keep getting interrupted."

She shrugged. "So, tell me now."

He took a deep breath. "Somehow you came to believe that—"

"Jack?" Another woman approached from behind her. Her voice sent a wave of sadness through Layla, and she prayed she was wrong.

The woman passed her chair, leaning down to kiss Jack's cheek. Even from behind, Layla recognized her. Her hair was pulled back in a tawny chignon, her posture perfect, her gait, graceful.

Connie.

"Connie, may I introduce ..."

Connie turned as he spoke.

"Layla," She and Jack said in unison.

"You know each other?" all three said simultaneously. Three strikes. Third time was the charm. Three witches in Macbeth. What was it about three? Layla would have liked to have gone somewhere quiet to take time ponder that. Anywhere but here. She stared at her cooling bowl of soup.

"Yes, we certainly do know each other." Connie spoke softly, barely audible above the din of other conversations, the clatter of forks against plates.

For Layla, her words were searing, focused, like a shout echoing through a tube. She nodded but ignored them both, still staring at her plate. Everything—everyone—she'd avoided for the past three years was personified by the woman staring at her. Every ounce of pain, every memory of humiliation.

A sinkhole would be welcome now, or an earthquake, or aliens landing on the roof of the restaurant. But Connie's presence trapped her as surely as if she were tied to the chair.

"Layla, my God, are you all right? I saw the news."

Connie's concern pierced her heart. Layla closed her eyes. *Please, just go away.*

"I've tried calling." Connie reached toward her.

Layla stiffened. She shook her head. "No. Please, Connie. I can't."

Connie turned to Jack, who took her hand and squeezed it. "I'll see you next time I'm in the emergency room."

"Okay," she whispered as she wiped at her eye.

What little soup Layla had eaten flip-flopped in her stomach. *The blonde was bad enough, all floozy and cute. But Connie ...*

She sensed rather than saw her leave and took a deep breath.

Jack let out a low whistle. "And you thought I was rude to the waiter."

She scowled at him, then slid her gaze to a cozy couple sitting next to each other on the same side of their table. The guy had his hand on his girlfriend's thigh and his eyes on a cute waitress. She snorted, then covered her mouth. *Oh nice—real ladylike.*

"Connie caught me by surprise."

"I'll try never to do that."

"That would imply I'll ever see you again. Which I doubt." *Did his eyes actually freaking twinkle?*

"Never say never."

"Look. This was not a good idea despite what my father thought." She dug into her purse extracting a leather wallet, worn around the seams. "I'm exhausted after the last two days."

Jack held up his hand. "I'll get this."

"I pay my own way." Pulling out three twenties, she tucked them next to her half-full soup bowl.

"At least tell me why you and Connie are enemies."

She stood. "We're not. We're best friends."

EIGHT

Jack watched Layla march out of the restaurant, mindful of other men watching as well. Damn, she was a tough nut to crack. What man would take on that challenge? *You would, dummy.* He rubbed his shoulder. If that's how she treated her best friend, how would she treat any man in her life? No wonder she was single.

Yet the interplay between Layla and her best friend intrigued him. On the surface she acted so cold, but why? Anger or hurt? Look at how she treated her father. With Clarence, she was kind, there was a softness about her. He'd even seen a glimmer of it as she sat opposite him at the table tonight.

Layla's love for her mother and Clarence, her care for him—those weren't qualities of a cruel person.

She wasn't the cold-hearted woman she portrayed. She wasn't shunning Connie; she was shrinking from her. For all her bluster, she was afraid. Of what? That Connie was a doctor?

Resting his chin in his hand, he stared at the flickering candle. In the candlelight her face had looked delicate, her skin so smooth. More than once, he'd found himself tracing an imaginary line from her chin up to her high cheekbones that were, what—

rosy? —in the candlelight. He'd liked the way her dark brows arced above her deep-set eyes.

He sat up and looked around. He had to knock it off. This woman was trouble from the word "go." She didn't want him around, so he wouldn't waste his time thinking about her. *Done with you, Layla. Good riddance.*

When the waiter placed a plate loaded with a sizzling ribeye before him, Jack pushed it away, no longer hungry.

"Would the lady like me to keep her plate warm until she returns?" The waiter held a plate above Layla's place.

"No. Would you please box these up to go?"

The man raised his eyebrows but lowered his gaze discreetly. "Of course, sir. I'll cork the wine bottle so you can take that as well."

"Damn."

"You don't want the wine, sir?"

"No. I mean yes, yes, cork it to go. I just realized I've forgotten something."

The man smirked. "An anniversary or birthday? I could add a bottle of champagne and chocolate truffles."

Jack frowned at him. "What?"

"The lady left. I thought perhaps ..."

Jack waved a hand dismissively. "No, I hardly know her. I just forgot to tell her I'm not a doctor."

The waiter's eyebrows shot up almost to his hairline.

JACK DROVE HOME SLOWLY. He needed to forget about her. Layla. Clapton was right. She could have him begging, darlin', please in a heartbeat. Time to run in the opposite direction.

Up ahead flashing lights signaled a traffic tie-up that would probably detour him a couple blocks out of his way. As he neared, a patrol car straddled the road, the officer directing traffic around the scene of an accident. This cop must have been first on the scene. The front of a dark brown SUV crumpled into a large oak, metal folded like an accordion from the bumper to the windshield.

Layla drove a dark brown SUV. He'd thought it funny when he saw it. Like she was a soccer mom or something. Then he'd spotted the customized access for a wheelchair. For Clarence.

Pulling off the side of the road, he rushed to the SUV. He flashed his ID badge at the cop. "EMT."

A look of relief swept over the young cop's face and he stepped aside. "Glad you're here."

The soup Jack had eaten threatened to make a reappearance. He ran to the driver's door and peered in.

A boy about sixteen was crushed into the airbag sandwiched by the seat and the crumpled front end. The steel frame along the door was bent, trapping him like a cage. Blood oozed from his nose; his closed eyes didn't react to Jack's voice.

Jack raised his gaze to the passenger seat, where a man in his early forties stared at the ceiling of the car. His airbag was all that kept him upright. His expression looked like he'd just walked into a surprise birthday party thrown for him. He would not celebrate any more birthdays.

Jack's stomach surged up his esophagus, and he fought it down. *This is today. This is today.* His mantra when accidents looked like this one.

He pressed his index and middle fingers against the teen's carotid artery, relieved to feel a pulse.

"We've got it from here, mister." A firm hand gripped his right shoulder.

Jack pivoted away from it. Dull throbbing radiated up his neck and along his spine.

"Oh, geez, I didn't see it was you, Jack." Steve Warczynski patted the shoulder he'd grabbed. "Sorry about that. Ambulance is right behind us. What do we have here?"

"Looks like one dead, one critical." Jack didn't move. He was transfixed by the scene, so similar to the one from sixteen years ago. On the console between the two victims, he spotted a cell phone grasped in the teen's hand. It was open with a text showing. A text that hadn't been sent. He hated taking comfort from that.

This is today. This is today.

Jack had hated his dad at age sixteen. How often had he wished him dead? Especially when he went after Mom or his little brother. Dad drank too much and hit too hard. Still, Jack had known Dad loved him.

They were heading to the liquor store that night, and he was driving because Dad was already tipsy. The November sun sat low in the dusky sky, blinding the driver heading west. He ran the stop sign. Jack had been driving only a few months and wasn't able to swerve out of the way. They got hit broadside.

He tried to help Dad, tried to administer the CPR he'd learned in health class. But his shoulder was dislocated by the impact, his humerus bone broken. He couldn't apply the necessary pressure to save Dad's life.

Every ache in his shoulder, every car accident call he answered brought the image of Dad's last breath to his mind.

Jack rose, his knees wobbly—probably from kneeling so long. Though he hadn't been kneeling that long. Must have been in a weird position.

"They're bringing the jaws of life." His friend Steve took off his firefighter's hat and ran his hand through his thick hair. At six foot four, he towered over Jack. "C'mon, buddy. There's nothing you can do right now. I'll take it from here. Aren't you off duty?"

"Yeah. I just finished dinner—well, almost dinner at Fulton Street Bistro. It didn't end well." *Stop babbling.*

"You okay, man?"

Jack rubbed the back of his neck. "Yeah. Shook me up when I saw this accident ..."

Steve scrunched his face. "Really? You've been doing this a long time. I've never seen you rattled before. You're always steady Eddy."

"I'll leave you to it. See ya'." Jack hurried to his truck, trying to still his trembling. *Not always, Steve. Car accidents get me every time. Every damn time.* And now, apparently, car accidents involving a brown SUV got him even worse. He arced his arm out and rotated it, loosening the shoulder muscles. Releasing his past, until the next time.

NINE

Layla's hands shook as she inserted the key into the lock of her condo door. How could this much disruption hit her in such a short time? First the damn envelope full of whatever. Then an overnight stay at the hospital, this doctor inserting himself into her life, and Connie showing up. All Layla wanted was a hot bath and her own bed.

She groaned at the knock on the door. She looked at the clock and scowled at "Seth Thomas." Was it only eight o'clock? Had she still been in the hospital only five hours earlier? "God," she moaned, tilting her head back and closing her eyes.

The knock sounded again.

No one came to visit. She doubted people she worked with had any idea where she lived. And she like it that way. There was no one she wanted to see right now even if they had known how to find her. Except one person.

Knock, knock.

"I know you're in there Layla, now open up this door."

Miss Ida.

Despite the desire to be a turtle and disappear into her shell, she smiled. She swung open the door to the smell of pot roast and inhaled deeply.

"You temptress."

"Don't try sneakin' in and lockin' your door before I can check on you."

Layla could spot a false friend in the course of a brief conversation, but Miss Ida was the real deal. The day Layla moved into the condo across the hall from her, Miss Ida had brought her a four-course meal. If her charm hadn't won her over, her five-star cooking did. Before she retired, Miss Ida had owned one of the most popular restaurants in Grand Rapids.

"Thanks, Miss Ida." Layla forced a smile, the energy sapping the little strength she still possessed. One kind word and she was in danger of blubbering.

Miss Ida narrowed her eyes. "Honey, you look like you got dragged through Target on Black Friday and you didn't end up with the Doorbuster Deal. What's goin' on?" The words floated behind Miss Ida with the aroma of onions, spices, and roasted vegetables as she carried the hot dish to the table in the kitchen. Kitchen was a generous term for what was basically a nook at the end of the living room. Setting down the plate, she spun and pointed at Layla. "And you didn't come home last night. Please tell me you were at some man's apartment doing the wild thing."

Dr. Jack Trenton.

Layla opened her mouth and then closed it like a fish.

"Well, it's about damn time! You need a little lovin' in your life." Under her breath she said, "More than a little would sweeten you right up." She jangled around the silverware drawer, pulling out a knife and fork, setting them beside the plate she'd brought.

Layla shook her head, as much to clear it as to respond. "Last night was incredible ..." She'd let her friend wonder for a minute. "Noisy, no sleep, and lots of action."

Miss Ida brightened.

"But it had nothing to do with wild sex. Or any sex."

Miss Ida frowned, one hand on her hip. "You know you need that, right? To stay healthy. Sleep, food, exercise, sex. I could write you a prescription if it would help."

"I spent the night in the hospital."

Miss Ida's hand flew to her heart. "Oh no!"

Layla leaned against the counter, eyeing the steaming pot roast dripping in gravy. The roasted rosemary potatoes and carrots called her name. She'd had no appetite at the Fulton Street Bistro, but these aromas changed her mind. "Maybe I'll eat a little." She sat at the table.

"Well, while you do, you'd best tell me what happened to put you in the hospital." Miss Ida plopped into the other chair.

"You obviously didn't watch the news last night."

"I worked the soup supper at church last night. Too tired to stay up until 11 o'clock." Miss Ida narrowed her eyes. "Didn't have time for the news today. Why. What happened? You can tell me."

Layla could tell her. This was the only place she would allow someone in besides Dad. Miss Ida had wormed her way into Layla's heart, and nurtured it as if she were her own daughter.

But as she explained what had happened at the office, she edited the account to alleviate any anxiety on Miss Ida's part. There was no reason to mention the hazmat guy or the fear she'd seen on her own face reflected in his mask. After all, he was long gone.

"Someone tried to ki...hurt you?"

Layla waved a hand. "No, I think it was a practical joke. Somebody's idea of a prank. Who knows, maybe they wanted to get out of work for a while and I was an easy target."

Miss Ida frowned, pointing a finger at her. "You need to take this seriously. Let me call Isaiah and have him file a report."

"Thanks, but don't bother your son. I've already filed a report with the police. A Detective Smythe followed up with an interview, and I couldn't offer him any help. It ticked him off."

"Promise me you'll be extra careful."

Nodding, Layla rubbed her eyes. "I promise."

Miss Ida caressed her cheek. "Honey, you need a good night's sleep." She rose and cleared Layla's place. From the pocket of her sweater, she produced a cloth napkin, which she placed in front of Layla and unfolded.

"Oh my God, Miss Ida. Snickerdoodles? And they're still warm?"

"Your favorite. Fresh from the oven." Miss Ida sat back down. "You need to build your strength. One of these nights will be noisy, sleepless, with lots of action." She dipped her head and looked at her as if over a pair of glasses. "And I'm not talking about any old hospital. Do you know what I mean?"

Layla dropped her head back and sighed. "You're trying harder to get me to have sex than my father tried to get me not to when I was a teenager." She sat forward and took her hand. "You are a sweetie. But you don't have to feed me all the time."

Miss Ida rose and packed up the plate and napkins she'd brought. "I miss cookin' for people, and you happen to be very convenient. Plus, you don't exactly know your way around a kitchen." She cast her a stern glance. "I assume your doctor recommended you take a couple days off?"

Layla nodded.

"Mm-hmm." Miss Ida dragged the word out like a gospel refrain. "And I assume you're going to ignore his or her orders. You get some rest now."

Dr. Trenton never gave her the order; the discharge nurse did. But she figured he had written the order. Or one of the myriad doctors who'd examined her.

Good-looking Dr. Trenton and his laughter (that she tried not to join), his kindness to her father (that she resented), and his magnetic attraction to women like Meredith. And even Connie.

Connie.

She dropped her head in her hands. Connie had sat beside her looking through their high school senior yearbook, sat beside her at their joint law school and medical school graduation party, sat beside her looking at dresses in bridal magazines.

Layla didn't hear the door close.

TEN

Wednesday, May 6

The gauntlet had a different vibe this morning, a subliminal thrumming of questions and curiosity that broke before her and rejoined in her wake. They hadn't expected her to return so soon. No one would dare ask her about the threat, that was certain.

Unlike other mornings, she looked them in the eyes. Did one of them hate her enough to do this? Was one of them hiding a smile? Was someone a good liar? She glanced at Seth's office, but it was empty. Dad was convinced Seth sent the letter. Maybe he didn't want to face her.

But Seth was no coward. The one thing she did admire about him was his drive to escape his tough upbringing in a poverty-stricken neighborhood, work his way through school, and earn a law degree. That had taken laser-focused determination. He was still rough around the edges, but he'd gotten what he'd wanted.

Angela greeted her with memos and messages as usual. What wasn't usual was the bright look in her eye—wary discernment or genuine concern? Layla wasn't sure. What she was sure of was that Angela could easily have slipped that envelope full of powder into an interoffice envelope and tucked in among her daily mail.

"We weren't expecting you to show up today, Lay—Miss Forrester."

I'm certain you weren't.

"How are you feeling?"

"I'm fine, thank you, Angela. What did I miss yesterday?" The pile of memos and messages was more than double its usual size.

"Yesterday we spent the morning putting your office back in order. The hazmat team scrubbed your office down thoroughly. I hope we put your things back in their proper place."

"We? We who?"

Angela's eyes changed from bright to dark and hooded. "Two of the paralegals and I."

Layla bit back her comment. *You know I don't want others in my office because of the confidential files.* "Thank you for handling that, Angela."

Angela straightened, almost smiled. "You're welcome."

Layla took the memos and messages. "I'll let you know if I need anything. In the future, except for you, I prefer no one enters my office while I'm not here."

The light faded from Angela's eyes. "Of course, Miss Forrester." The muscle in her jaw twitched.

When she entered her office, the usual sound from the overhead light buzzed, the usual traffic noise from Monroe St. murmured through the closed windows, and the chatter had picked up outside her door. But she shivered when she looked at her desk and held her breath.

Breathe.

Was it just two days ago? As she surveyed the office, she noticed several items in the wrong place. Her display screen was on the wrong side of the desk, her phone was in the center, the empty space for her laptop was to the left. She pursed her lips and closed the door.

Could Angela have sent the envelope? They didn't have a friendly relationship, but Layla treated her professionally and fairly. A good review and a generous raise, a gift at Christmas. Not a "let's get together for drinks" relationship. She didn't even do that with friends anymore.

What friends?

After rearranging her desk, Layla hunkered down to read a brief she was working on. This would take her mind off the threat and get her back on track. But the words blurred before her eyes. She reread sentences, none of them making sense. Her concentration was shot, and she almost welcomed whoever had knocked and opened her door, waiting.

Almost welcomed, until she looked up and saw Seth, hands on the doorframe, body leaning in, eyes narrowed. For a moment his face turned into a clock, then morphed back to his own. She blinked.

"Yes? How can I help you, Seth?" Her words were brusque.

"Sorry to bother you, Miss Forrester." He slid her name out like an accusation. "I came by to see how you're feeling. I didn't mean to disturb you."

Was that a glint in his eye? His concern sounded thin, and she guessed he'd come to gloat.

"Oh, please, Seth. Let it go." She returned to her case, dismissing him. She didn't have to look up to know he was still there.

He closed the door and sat down before she could object. She looked up as he dropped a file on her desk and set his reading glasses on top of it.

"I'm trying to be nice, and you just blow me off." He scowled at her.

"I'm fine. Thank you for your concern." She cocked her head and stared at him. "Now will you leave?"

He snorted. "Just like when we was together. Miss Ice Queen ...."

She fought the urge to correct his grammar, a habit he slipped into from his years in a tough neighborhood.

"... though I know you can be hotter than hell."

Layla fought the warmth that crept from her neck to her cheeks. Their lovemaking had been torrid, from a release of tension more than passionate love. In their work as attorneys with the firm, the stress was tangible. Often it was make-up sex after yet another argument. She understood why corporations had a no fraternizing policy. It just screwed things up—literally and figuratively.

"Stop ..." she growled.

"No, I'm not gonna stop. You think everything is yours for the taking. Well, guess what, other people are deserving, too."

"I don't even know who you are right now." She glared at him.

He snorted. "I just wanted to show my sincere concern for you."

"Sincere concern? Really? If that envelope hadn't been full of mostly powder, I could be dead and you'd be sitting in this chair."

He leapt to his feet, knocking over his chair. "Son of a bitch! You think I had anything to do with that?"

"I didn't say that."

"You didn't have to." He pressed his hands on her desk, his knuckles white with the pressure, and leaned toward her. "Just because you have a heart of stone, don't assume everyone else does. You probably have a spreadsheet with the names of all the people you suspect. I have no doubt I'm at the top of that very long list. Wake up, Layla. Everyone's not out to get you. Everyone isn't like Mark Ross."

Her head jerked back as if she'd been slapped. "That was a low blow, Seth."

"That's all you understand. Cruelty and insults. Now it's your turn to take it."

He stormed out, slamming the door behind him.

As she stared at the door she inhaled deeply, stemming her anger at the sting of his words.

It didn't matter. Nothing mattered except Dad.

The door reopened.

"What?" Layla barked.

Angela entered with a steaming cup of coffee. With hazelnut creamer. Just the way Layla liked it.

Layla wiped at her eyes. "Thank you, Angela."

"Ms. Forrester, you look pale. Maybe—"

"I'm fine."

Angela stiffened. "Of course."

The door closed a bit louder than usual.

Layla twitched her mouth to the side. *I didn't have to be so sharp with her. She was just being nice. But I know where being nice leads.*

She could almost smell the white roses and calla lilies in her bouquet and see Connie gliding down the aisle before her. Dad held her arm, ready to escort her down the aisle using just his cane.

Mark stood beside the priest, stone-faced. When she reached halfway, he spun and ran to the sacristy.

Nerves, she'd thought. And Dad had escorted her the rest of the way to the altar.

The priest smiled at her and glanced toward the sacristy.

They waited. And waited. Guests shifted in their seats, and whispers began softly, then buzzed like a swarm of bees.

They heard the side door to the church open and close. All of them heard it as it echoed through the space. The whispers died down, and the weight of one hundred pairs of sympathetic eyes burned into her back. Weighing her down as if each were a boulder.

That's where niceness led. That's where love led. And she was never going back.

ELEVEN

Jack stared at his cards. All spades with both black jacks—he had a loner euchre hand. He tried to look bored. He loved this game. The strategy, the skill, and the plain dumb luck. Between calls at the fire station, he played euchre with Steve Warczynski and whichever other two guys were lucky enough to sit at the table.

"You must have a dynamite hand, Trenton."

Jack scoffed. "What, these cards?"

"You always get that dumbass look on your face when you're holding good cards. So, I'm going to order my partner to pick up that ten of hearts."

"You dick." Jack slapped his cards on the table. "Okay, smartass, go it alone."

"I think I will." Steve played both red jacks and took the first two tricks. Then he led the king of spades, and Jack played the ace, taking the trick. He played the queen of spades, and the other three were void. He took the last trick with the jack of spades.

"Euchred!" Jack pumped his fist. "Two points for us." He

flipped over his two of spades score card, resting it on top of the face-down three.

"Better two than four." Steve scooped up the cards.

"Hey, I count this a win."

"Seriously, Jack. You need to work on your poker face."

Jack punched him in the arm. "You—"

The clanging of the fire alarm interrupted him, and chairs screeched along the wood floor as men hurried to their vehicles.

Jack's hands shook from all the coffee he'd been drinking to make up for the sleepless night. An early trip to the gym and a hearty breakfast at Mario's helped stave off fatigue this morning, too. He moved at full speed now as he and his partner careened down the road, siren blaring. Talking was impossible over the noise, so he concentrated on driving. Though one thought niggled his brain.

The one thing he hadn't done yet today was call Layla. Now he was procrastinating. The longer she thought he was a doctor, the harder it would be to correct her misconception. Maybe it wasn't even an issue. Maybe he'd never see her again.

Ouch. He didn't like that thought.

He'd promised Clarence he'd come by and play cribbage tomorrow when his shift ended at three. He could get a couple games in and be out of there before she showed up for her daily visit. If he timed things right, he'd never have to face her and tell her she was mistaken. His gut told him she wasn't the kind of woman who wanted to be told she was mistaken.

He followed the fire truck around a corner, dodging a distracted motorist who almost sideswiped him. "Jesus," he whispered, part curse, part prayer. Up ahead, the accident slowed traffic. Three cars, the front of the compact crushed up to the windshield. He hated crashes. He massaged his shoulder. He hated the grief of the victims. He hated the memories that came unbidden.

He parked next to the crushed car, protecting it from distracted drivers and rubbernecking passers-by. The woman in the driver's seat was screaming, "My baby! My baby!"

Glancing into the back seat, he spotted a toddler strapped in a car seat. Blood oozed out from the child's clenched fists, but a loud wailing signaled he was alive. Glass covered the inside of the car, reaching back to the child.

"Time to get to work." Steve's grim statement echoed his thoughts.

He heaved a sigh. This car looked the worst of the three, and, apparently, these victims would survive.

He always counted that a win.

LAYLA STARED out her window at the clouds scudding through the bluest sky she'd ever seen. The same blue as his eyes. She brushed her hair back, banishing the image. She'd planned to call the hospital and tell Dr. Jack Trenton to stay out of her life and away from her father, but she hadn't picked up the phone yet.

Dad enjoyed his company. All that mattered to her was Dad's happiness and comfort, so if the good doctor wanted to visit, who was she to interfere? Why did this bother her so?

I'm jealous. She wanted to be the only person Dad needed. It was selfish and juvenile. Just because she'd banished all her friends for the last three years didn't mean Dad had to.

The image of Jack's blue eyes returned, and the way his tan accentuated the laugh lines that crinkled at the corners. His quick smile and infectious laugh. She crossed her arms. But he didn't need to be hanging around Dad. And he had plenty of attention from other women; he didn't need more. Not that she intended to give him attention. He may be kind, but he was danger wrapped in one gorgeous package.

It's not just jealousy of Dad that makes you want to keep him away, is it?

Another knock. She dropped her head back and looked at the ceiling. Now what?

"Come in."

"Morning, Miss Forrester." Jimmy entered with her mail.

She groaned inwardly at the stack he carried, but she couldn't help but smile back at Jimmy. Then she studied him. He wore the same shirt he'd had on the other day, but it was rumpled with a ketchup stain on one sleeve. And his bowtie was missing.

"Hey, Jimmy. How is Detroit doing today?"

"They're on a three-day winning streak." He'd brightened, but he didn't speak in his usual cheery tone.

"I would think you'd be very happy about that."

Jimmy shuffled the mail in his hands, not looking at her. "I am ... I am happy about that."

"They must have known you were watching out for them."

His laugh made her laugh. God, it felt good to laugh.

"You're so funny, Miss Forrester."

"I watched the game the other night while I was in the ..." He didn't need to know about that.

His face crumpled. "The hospital. I know you were there. I'm ... I'm so sorry. Are you still sick?"

"No, no! I'm fine. Look at me!" She held her arms up, elbows bent at ninety degrees, fists clenched, like she was showing off her muscles.

"You look beautiful." His face turned crimson.

Her heart melted. At least someone thought she was beautiful. She blinked the mist out of her eyes. "Why, thank you, Jimmy."

He set the mail on her desk. "Right where you like it."

Her stomach did flip-flops, and she sat back as if he'd set down a rattlesnake.

"Are you okay, Miss Forrester?" He reached out to her, revealing another red ketchup stain on the cuff of his shirt. "There's nothing bad in this mail. I didn't let anybody put anything bad in it."

"Yes, I'm okay. Thanks, Jimmy." She pointed to the stain. "Looks like you were dipping some French fries." She smiled up at him.

His smile disappeared, and he smoothed his rumpled shirt. He reached up to straighten his absent bow tie, then dropped his hands to his sides. His lower lip trembled.

"I had to wear this shirt again. I ... I didn't have another one to ... to ... to wear."

She took his hand. "That's okay, Jimmy. Is the washing machine at the group home broken?"

"We don't have a washing machine at home."

A low thrumming whirred in her gut.

"Why not, Jimmy? I thought your home had a big washing machine." She didn't want to hear his answer. She had a good idea what he was about to say.

"Oh, no, not *that* home, at our house."

Her blood ran cold. He was back with his father.

"What do you mean, Jimmy?"

He brightened. "Trevor came home from jail. He came to work to see me the other day, and I showed him the mailroom where I work, and later we got all of my stuff from that other place."

He said the last words with disdain, echoing, she was certain, Trevor's assessment.

"Trevor said I belong at home with my family."

Trevor cared about Jimmy. Maybe this would be all right, though judging by Jimmy's appearance, she wasn't convinced.

"High five, Miss Forrester." He held up his hand, and Layla slapped it.

"High five, Jimmy. You made my day."

He chuckled. "Oh, you always say that."

"Because I always mean it."

"Have a good day." He stood, looking at her.

"You, too. See ya."

"See ya." He stopped and turned back. "Oh, and Trevor says hi."

Her heart raced and cold ran through her.

"What did you say?" she whispered.

"Trevor told me to tell you, 'Hi.' See you tomorrow, Miss Forrester." His steps were slow as he left.

Trevor, who cursed her after his sentence was read. "I'm not the only one who'll pay," he'd whispered as he passed her table on the way out of court.

She eyed the stack of mail, fighting off the sick feeling in her stomach. Would she find another threatening note? Would she find another envelope filled with powder—this time more potent?

Taking a deep breath—in case she needed to not breathe—she reached for the first envelope. There was no letter addressed "Layla Forrester, Bitch." There was nothing out of the ordinary. When she finished the last piece of correspondence, she breathed deeply. No life-threatening messages today—so far. She could get on with her life.

Maybe she could stop thinking about Trevor and his threat.

Hoping to refocus on the ordinary, she checked her planner. *Call Dr. Trenton.*

Ugh. Maybe she should make that phone call to the hospital now. But did she really want to face talking to Jack? Jimmy's news was unsettling. Tackling the mail had wrung her out. She'd call later. Or did she need to call at all? There was no reason for him to come back into her life ... hers and Dad's, that is. Maybe just let things fade away.

What she really needed to tackle was this threat. Maybe someone thought it was a prank, but its effect weighed on her.

And now she could add Trevor to the list of suspects. She searched her purse for Detective Smythe's number.

TWELVE

Jack had always considered himself an above average cribbage player, but Clarence was beating the pants off him.

"Fifteen two, fifteen four ..." Clarence once again counted up his points. His glee at winning was matched only by his superior strategy.

"I might have to ask for a new deck of cards," Jack teased as Clarence moved his peg along the hand-carved maple cribbage board.

"We've already switched to a new one, Jack. Deal. I'm only four pegs away from beating you ... again."

Jack glanced at the clock on the wall. Five o'clock. He'd planned to bug out by four thirty to eliminate any possibility of running into Layla, though a part of him had readily agreed to another game when Clarence challenged him.

"You can stop shuffling, Jack. It's not going to change your luck." Clarence chortled.

"I'm watching you, Forrester. You'd better not be cheating."

"Don't have to."

"I'll drink to that." Jack raised his beer bottle, and Clarence tapped it with his own.

"Ready for another beer?"

Jack shook his head. "No. Just one. Gotta drive home." He dealt the cards.

The door opened, and Jack caught a hint of Layla's perfume. *Shit. Caught, like a kid with his hand in the cookie jar.*

"Hi, honey. I'm beating Jack's butt in cribbage."

Jack turned to see her standing in the doorway, her face a thundercloud.

Damn. I should have called her.

LAYLA FROZE IN THE DOORWAY. *That's our special game.* This is what she got for not making that phone call today. She was sure flames were shooting out the top of her head.

"What are you doing here?" She frowned at Jack.

"Now, honey, Jack has a right to be here. He came by to challenge me to a game or two of cribbage," Clarence wheedled—he always wheedled when he teased. His eyes lit up with delight.

"I see that." She wanted to sweep the cards off the table and send them flying, cribbage board and all. She crossed her arms. Why did her heart wrench like this?

What was she really upset about? Jack being here with Dad? Or Jack being here at all?

Jack set down the deck of cards. "I'd better go."

"Yes." Her nails dug into her fists. If she were honest, she'd admit part of her wanted him to stay. But having him around was too dangerous; she could feel her resolve diminishing already. A man in her life was not in the plan and never would be.

Jack stood. "Layla, I need to talk to you." He reached for her hand.

She pulled away. "There's nothing for us to talk about."

"But..."

She stepped out of his path to the door.

He stood toe to toe with her. The scent of sandalwood drifted to her, and she tried not to breathe, or she'd reverse her command. She was holding her breath a lot lately. She stared at the bridge of his nose, not daring to look into his ocean-blue eyes. What was it with this guy? She wanted him out. She wanted him, period.

"You know, I've been trying to tell you something—the truth about something, but obviously you just don't care." He turned to Clarence. "Good game, Clarence. Good-bye." He stormed out.

Dad's face flushed scarlet, his brows jabbed down. Uh-oh. She hadn't seen this look on his face since high school. The word *grounded* came to mind, and her heart thumped. Straightening, she lifted her chin. "What?"

"Damn it, Layla, why did you do that?" Clarence thundered.

"I don't want him around. He's too ..."

"Attractive? Threatening? What the hell is wrong with you?"

How could she tell Dad that she was jealous?

"He's a good guy. We were having a great game." He swept his arm above the table where the cards and cribbage board spread out.

"But *we* always play cribbage, Dad." *Oh my God, I sound like a whining teenager.* She looked away.

"Yes, when you have time." He clamped his mouth shut.

His words stung.

"I visit every day."

He wiped a hand along his balding head, then scratched at the fringe of hair that ran along the sides. "And I appreciate that. I know how busy your job keeps you, and I really do appreciate that you take the time to visit every day. But you can't be my only company. That's not fair to you, and it's not fair to me. Besides, it's different with a guy ... I can't explain it.

It's like you and Connie getting together. I can't take her place."

His words hit like scattershot, reaching so many vulnerable places. She brushed aside a strand of hair and with it the pain of his words.

"Layla." Her name sounded like a prayer. He held out his arms.

She knelt beside his chair and he held her, stroking her hair. Then he kissed the top of her head. "I love you, Sliver."

"Love you, too, Dad." She closed her eyes. She couldn't bother Dad with her concerns. But wondering where the next threat would come from stretched her nerves taut. She needed to get hold of herself. No coward was going to get under her skin.

As if reading her mind, he asked, "Have you found out who sent that powder stuff to you? Was it that Thomas guy?"

She pushed away and stood. "I don't know. The police said they would investigate, but I haven't heard anything. There's probably nothing to find. Somebody was a jerk, and the joke backfired." Detective Smythe had reported back that there were no prints or identifying marks on the envelope. As far as Trevor went, getting out of jail didn't constitute a crime.

He took her hand. "I worry about you, Sliver."

She sat in the chair Jack had vacated, still warm from his body heat. She brushed away another imaginary strand of hair, dismissing that awareness.

Dad looked at her with a gleam in his eye. "Have time for a game?"

No, she had to appear in court at eight o'clock the next morning, and she'd planned to review her case notes and call it an early night to make up for the previous night's loss of sleep.

"Of course. If you think you can win." She cast him a wicked smile.

Dad won the cut and took the deck of cards. He shuffled

them and dealt the hand. Studying his cards, he said, "I'm going to invite him back."

She took a deep breath. "I know." She held a deuce, a four, a five, two sixes, and a jack. Should she keep the jack or throw him —it—to Dad?

How was she going to play this?

———

DAD STICKING up for Jack hurt. As she left Brookside, she focused on the floor, one step in front of the other, so she didn't see someone entering the door when she pushed it to exit.

"Geez, watch out! Oh, it's you." Dwayne Brown, Crystal's brother, stood in her way.

Layla hadn't seen him since the night he'd brought Dad the wrong meds. Now he towered over her, the front of his dirty jacket in her face.

They stood in the vestibule between the inner and outer doors. Layla had heard the inner one click as it locked behind her.

She straightened to her full height. "Sorry, I didn't see you." She'd never expected to see him again either.

"Right." His large frame blocked her path.

She tried to take a deep breath to tamp down the alarm that rose within, but he smelled of stale beer and cigarettes. One deep breath and she'd gag. "Excuse me."

"Oh, am I in your way?" His sneer sent shivers along her spine.

She looked him in the eye. "Yes. And I'm in your way. So, unless you move, neither of us will get to where we want to go."

He folded his arms and planted his feet.

She folded her arms and held his gaze.

A *whoosh* sounded as the door behind her opened, bumping her closer to him.

"What the hell are you doing, Dwayne?" Crystal stood behind her.

Keeping his gaze fixed on Layla, he grunted. "Ms. Forrester here is blocking my way and won't move."

"Oh, geez, grow up. Move your fat ass."

His gaze slid to his sister. "She blocks me everywhere I go." He fixed Layla with a flinty stare.

She didn't move.

"Move it, Dwayne. I'm starving."

He turned and slammed out the door.

Layla turned to her. "Thanks."

Crystal snorted. "I didn't do it for you. I am starving. Far as I'm concerned, you can go to hell." She pushed past her.

THIRTEEN

The hands on her clock, partly covering the Seth Thomas logo, announced eight thirty when Layla opened her apartment door. This day had been two weeks long. She kicked off her heels, dropped her laptop on her chair, and headed toward the refrigerator where a newly opened bottle of moscato d'Asti awaited her.

Once she settled into her favorite lumpy chair, her laptop opened to case file notes, she took a sip of wine and reached for the plate of Muenster cheese and Ritz crackers. A pairing of cheese and crackers almost reached her mouth when a knock sounded.

Gathering up the laptop, she placed it on the cherry coffee table and padded to the door before Miss Ida could call out, "I know you're in there, Layla."

When she opened the door, Miss Ida held out a crock of soup. "Minestrone. Your favorite." She cocked her head, waiting for Layla to take the soup. Once she did, Miss Ida pushed past her and spotted the wineglass. "Is that your fancy-ass wine with bubbles?"

Layla chuckled. "Yes. And there's plenty for both of us."

"Must be nice to be able to afford fancy-ass wine." Miss Ida couldn't keep a straight face.

"You know how I throw my money around."

"I know it's one of your few luxuries. I also know you buy your Gucci bags and Chanel suits at online garage sales and discount sites. And live here instead of a high-priced condo downtown." She eased down on the sofa.

Layla handed her a generous pour.

"Woo-eee! That'll make me sleep tonight."

"I wish I could sleep at night." Layla curled up in her chair, nestling the crock of soup against her chest.

"Bad dreams?"

Layla nodded.

"After what you've been through, it's no wonder." Miss Ida sipped her moscato and gave her a sidelong glance. "If you tell someone, the dreams have less power, and sometimes they fade away."

Layla looked into her glass, watching miniscule bubbles slide along the glass to the surface of her wine. "There's one especially bad dream." Why did this dream bother her more than the actual threat?

Because the threat was a prank that backfired, but the reality of this dream would never be erased.

Miss Ida waited.

"The guy who came into my office after I opened the envelope."

Miss Ida set her glass on the end table and folded her hands.

Layla shook her head, trying to erase the image. "I couldn't see his face through the visor..." She met Miss Ida's gaze. Layla's heart warmed at the comfort—no, the love—her gaze conveyed. And Miss Ida was listening ... truly listening. The usual "danger" sign that flashed in her mind when she got close to exposing her feelings to someone did not flash. Didn't even appear. She took a deep breath.

"... but I could see my face reflected in it."

Miss Ida pursed her lips, nodding slightly.

"I was so afraid. So scared. I felt like a child who lost ... was lost." She turned her wineglass in circles. "He saw how afraid I was."

"That hurt."

Miss Ida got her. Even though Layla almost threw the casserole at Miss Ida the day she moved in, Miss Ida never gave up on her. Somehow, Layla's charade didn't fool her. Instead, she'd become a second mother.

"I hated that he saw me so vulnerable. I hated him. I'm glad I'll never see whoever he is again."

"Perfectly understandable. And you probably will never see him again. But I'm not sure you hate him. After all, it wasn't his fault that he was there to save your life."

Layla's gaze shot back to her. The anger that flashed within her dissolved into mirth as she recognized the truth in Miss Ida's words. They burst out laughing.

"Truth deserves another drink." Layla filled each of their glasses.

"Careful, I have to find my way home."

They laughed again.

"Thank you. You are such a gift to me." She took Miss Ida's hand. "I'm so glad I moved in here and not some high-priced condo downtown."

They clinked their glasses.

"I'm glad, too. Gives me somebody to cook for." She smiled, then looked serious. "Plus, I know it allows your father to live at Brookside." Miss Ida raised her glass in silent salute.

Layla shrugged. "He's everything to me. He needs good care. The best."

"And you'll do whatever it takes to make sure he gets it. Including being willing to take a promotion that you deserved but may put you in an uncomfortable position in the future. Has your boss, that Mr. Gage, propositioned you yet?"

"Not directly. I think he thinks he's being subtle for now."

"What are you gonna do when he makes his move?"

Layla sipped a spoonful of soup. What was she going to do? She'd deserved the promotion but couldn't ignore that Roland might expect an affair to be part of the bargain. If she turned him down, would he demote her? Fire her?

Comments he'd made edged on sexual harassment, but Roland took them just so far, couched in ambiguous terms. If she called him on them, he'd say her mind was in the gutter. If she refused him, he'd cook up some way to make her look incompetent. She tiptoed a fine line, but the promotion included a raise that made Dad's arrangements much more affordable. She'd been sick of Ramen noodles, and Miss Ida could only keep feeding her for so long.

"I'm positioning myself to avoid any alone time with him. I bring work home rather than work late hours. So far, my plan has worked. I wonder ..."

"I can see the wheels turning. What do you wonder?" Miss Ida took a long sip of her wine. "Mmm, mmm."

"This is a long stretch, but what if it was Roland who sent the threatening note?"

"Hmm... But why? What would he gain?"

Layla sipped more soup. "If he keeps me off balance, I might be grateful for his patronage no matter the cost."

"And if you weren't, he could try to fluster you so much you'd become distracted, and he could fire you for incompetency. You'll have to tread carefully." Miss Ida drained her wineglass and stood, eyeing the case notes filling the laptop screen. "Looks like someone is going to be up late tonight."

Layla sipped the last spoonful from soup crock and rose to take it out to the sink. "This soup was yummy. Thank you."

Miss Ida took the crock from her. "You just get to work and then to bed."

Layla kissed her cheek. "You don't have to feed me, you know."

Miss Ida wrapped her hand around Layla's wrist, her thumb easily reaching her middle finger. "Girl, I need to fatten you up. You need a little cushion for the pushin' when it's time for the wild thing."

Layla laughed, caressing her hand. "Miss Ida, you are corrupting my morals."

"No, I'm encouraging your sacral chakra."

As she closed and locked the door behind Miss Ida, Jack's image came to mind as it often had the last four days.

Maybe playing doctor would be fun.

FOURTEEN

Saturday, May 9

Layla tapped her foot to the music that serenaded the crowd attending Spring Fest. Since Roland's firm was a sponsor, they had a booth at Rosa Parks Circle. She'd volunteered to take the Saturday morning shift with Mariana, but Mariana had come down with the stomach flu, so she was on her own.

She inhaled the fresh spring air ... well, as fresh as it could be in downtown Grand Rapids. The morning had started out chilly, but now the May sun warmed her face and dazzled off the glass and metal surfaces along the street. The temperature had risen into the seventies, so she'd switched from hot coffee to a cool iced tea.

While Layla's occasional customers swooped in for a free keychain or hand sanitizer, ignoring her firm's literature, the woman in the next booth had been busy selling handmade jewelry. She had a lull right now.

"Would you mind keeping an eye on my booth while I run to the restroom?" Layla called to her.

"Sure! I'd be happy to." The woman smiled over the heads of two teens examining leather bracelets.

When she returned, customers again swarmed the woman's booth. *Good thing all our stuff was free.* She picked up her iced tea. As she brought the plastic cup to her lips, she saw something floating at the bottom of the glass. She dropped it, spilling the contents on the table. A dead mouse lay cradled on keyrings that would never be given away.

She jumped back. "Holy crap!" Then she spotted the scrawled writing on one of the firm's brochures: Hello, Bitch.

"What's up, Layla?"

She jumped again.

Seth stood behind her, his face calm, his words casual. What were the chances he'd just shown up? Was he going to gloat now?

"Did you do this?" She pointed to the table.

His brows arced down. "What?" He spotted the mouse

"I need to know if you're the person behind these threats."

His mouth gaped, and his face flushed. "Are you nuts? Do you really think I'd do this to you?"

He seemed sincere. But he could be lying, just as he lied about being with Angela while they were still dating. She could only imagine that pillow talk.

"I thought I knew the worst of you, but I was wrong. How you can accuse me of this ..."

"Well, you just happened to show up the moment I discovered another threat."

"I 'showed up' because my shift starts at noon." His face darkened, and his hands balled into fists. "And I *just* showed up. So I didn't have time to find a mouse and drown it in your damned drink." He leaned over her, veins sticking out in his neck, his face the color of a pickled beet.

She balanced against the table. She'd never been afraid of

Seth—he was all bluster—but at this moment, his anger shook her.

"You okay, Layla?"

She turned, bumping into Jack, his eyes blazing in Seth's direction.

"Yes. Yes, I'm okay."

Though Seth was taller, Jack's shoulders were broader and more muscled. He leaned forward, and she thought of two male elk she'd seen on The Discovery Channel.

"Seth Thomas, this is Dr. Jack Trenton. He took care of me in the hospital after my first threat." She stressed the last two words.

Seth's nostrils flared, and he bunched his fists. He said nothing, but he grunted. She tried to remember if the male elk grunted like that.

Jack put his arm around Layla's shoulders. Male elk sheltering the female.

"I'd say it's nice to meet you, but this didn't sound very friendly."

Seth poked his chin at her. "I'm being accused of a serious offense here, and I don't particularly like it."

"I didn't accuse you, Seth. I was just performing an inquiry into the crime." She angled away from Jack.

"What crime is that?" Jack slid his arm off her shoulders.

Seth poked his chin toward the table. "Mouse in her drink."

Jack whistled. "That's nasty."

"And don't forget the fentanyl-laced letter." Layla crossed her arms.

Jack raised his eyebrows and whistled again. "So, whoever sent you the powder has now done this?"

"I don't know for certain, but it seems odd that a mouse would jump into my iced tea. And then there's this note." She pointed to it.

She studied Jack while he studied the note. His forehead

crinkled, and it was, well, endearing. She hated admitting that. His jaw twitched as he gently poked the mouse, a dribble of tea escaping its mouth. He examined the people at the next booth, then scanned the crowd, then squinted at Seth.

If Seth was behind these threats, she'd make sure he paid, and she didn't need Jack or anyone else's help making sure he did.

Seth, meanwhile, shifted from foot to foot. His fists were still clenched, his chin still poked out like a defiant eighth-grade boy.

Jack squinted up at him. "So, you didn't do this?"

There it was. Blunt and straight-up. Men handled things so well.

"Of course I didn't do this. Or the powder." His bass voice bellowed, and the shoppers at the jewelry booth glanced at him, some frowning, some amused. He turned on Layla. "Look, things didn't work out for us. Fine. You got the promotion. Fine. Am I pissed about all that? You bet I am. Would I do this?" His hand swept toward the mouse. Then he stepped closer, getting right in her face, and whispered hoarsely, "I would never do this to you."

She forced herself to stand her ground, not flinch, not back up a step. His words sounded sincere, but then so had his words when he'd denied sleeping with Angela. While the two of them were still dating. She planted her feet and straightened her shoulders, then she leaned into him, holding his gaze.

"I've heard your innocent pleas before, Seth. They turned out to be lies."

His nostrils flared, puffs of breath punching out. His eyes drilled into her. "Well, there's a long list of possible suspects, I imagine." He stepped back, nodded to Jack, turned on his heel, and stalked away.

She folded her arms, glaring at his back.

"I think he likes you."

She glanced at him out of the corner of her eye. "What?"

"Seth. I think he still carries a torch for you." Though he didn't smile, Jack's eyes danced with mischief.

"Are you nuts? And, by the way, what are you doing here?"

His eyebrows shot up. "So now you suspect me?"

"Well, this is certainly convenient. You just turning up like this."

He held up his index finger. "Number one, I didn't know you before Monday." He held up the next finger. "Number two, I came for the beer." He held up a third finger. "Number three, why add more suspects to your list? Seth said you have a long list already."

Damn, he was right. She clenched her teeth. Then she grabbed his arm. "Look." She pointed to a booth across from them.

Crystal and Dwayne Brown were sitting at a table drinking beer with a group of people.

"Isn't that the aide from Brookside? Who's the guy she's with?"

"That's Crystal's brother, Dwayne. He brought Dad the wrong meds one night. Dad only takes a few, but Dwayne handed him more than usual. Dad was focused on the Tigers game and almost popped them in his mouth before I stopped him. I reported Dwayne, and he got fired. I'm not really comfortable with his sister, Crystal, bringing Dad's food, but he says Crystal's fine, it was an accident, and not to worry."

"You don't think it was intentional, do you?"

Was it? She pondered that. "Probably not, but it was incompetent, and it could have had serious consequences for Dad." She looked back at Dwayne. "We just had a nasty encounter at Brookside the other night."

"I thought he got fired."

She stared at the siblings. "He was picking up Crystal. He

blocked me from leaving the building." Her eyes met Jack's. "He was very threatening."

She and Jack stared down at the mouse. Then Layla took it by the tail, dropped it in the cup, and threw it in the trash can. "Poor thing."

She fished out sanitizing wipes from the box of supplies, cleaned up the spilled tea, and threw away the wet keyrings. Jack picked up the note by a corner so she could wipe down the table. When she'd finished, she looked back at the group. Dwayne glanced up and caught her eye. He sneered.

"Damn," she whispered. She pitched the dirty wipe into the trash. "Oh, here comes Seth."

Seth stopped at the end of the table. "It's noon. Time for my shift."

"Great. Let's go report this to the police and then go to lunch." Jack took her arm and led her down the street.

She stared at him as if he'd just said, "Let's go rob a bank."

"You are nuts."

"You look a little peaked"—he said "peak-ed" like Grandma Jane used to say when she had the flu—"and food will help. Food always helps." He breathed a soft cluck out the side of his mouth and shook his head as he examined the note. "You are going to report this, right?"

Clouds floated in front of the sun, bringing a slight breeze. She shivered, then shrugged to mask it. "Report what? Anybody could have dropped that mouse in my tea."

"Yes..."

"But what? There's a but hanging out there." She stopped, hands on hips.

"Well, we certainly can't have butts hanging out."

"Seriously, what were you going to add?"

"But then there is this note and the powder."

She took the note from him. "Look, if whoever did this really

intended to hurt me, they would have done so by now." She
waved her arm, indicating the city. "See, they can find me
anywhere. This person is a cringing coward, and I don't plan to
give him the attention he's seeking or validate his attempt at
scaring me."

"But that mouse and this note sure looks like another threat.
And this guy could be more serious than you're giving him credit
for. You're a lawyer. Look at the evidence."

She wavered. He was right, but she was determined not to let
this creep control her. She would ignore him, dismiss him, and
he'd get tired and go away. Or maybe keep up the harassment, but
she doubted he'd have the courage to attack her directly.

He took her elbow. "C'mon. I'll buy you lunch. Decisions are
always easier on a full stomach." He steered her toward the
corner.

She pulled back. "Jack, I really don't want to sit in some
restaurant while various women come up to bat their eyes at
you."

He stopped and grinned.

She hated how his eyes sparkled—there was no other word
for it—when he teased her. She hated how she turned warm and
gooey inside when he did. She hated it, and hoped he'd do it
again.

"No batting women, I promise. And I'm buying." He led her
down the street to a hot dog stand with a Dogs on Monroe sign.

She laughed.

At the sound, he turned and smiled at her. "You *can* laugh.
Proved me wrong again."

She slapped his shoulder. "It's like Nessie, the Loch Ness
Monster. Don't blink or you'll miss it." Despite the disquiet of the
mouse incident, lightness filled her. Could she say happiness?
Don't get carried away. You're just weak from hunger. She
glanced at Jack. But what kind of hunger?

Jack ordered a chili dog with extra hot sauce. Layla ordered a plain dog with mustard and relish. She wore ecru capris and a pale yellow blouse, and chili sauce did not blend well with either.

The sun had returned and warmed them as they strolled toward the river and found an empty bench. She savored the sun on her face, the warmth, the brightness. She needed to get outside more often now that spring had arrived.

Jack took off his jacket and spread it out. "*Madame,*" he said in a passable French accent as he bowed slightly, indicating her seat.

"Aren't you the *gallant?*" she returned in an equally passable French accent... if one were not French.

"Perhaps you need a *gallant* after all you've been through."

She bristled and stepped back. "I don't need anyone."

He held up one hand, palm facing out. "Got it. But you might need my jacket so you don't get your bu...pants dirty."

She frowned at his jacket lying innocently on the bench. *Just because you take him up on his jacket offer, doesn't mean you owe him anything.* "Thank you." She sat stiffly on the bench, careful not to move the jacket lest dirt get rubbed into it.

"The other option was to sit on my lap. My jacket is very happy." He took a bite of his chili dog.

She glared at him.

The corner of his mouth hitched. "To be of service, not because your bu... you're sitting on it." He wiped his mouth. "You can be a real pain, you know." He took another bite.

"You're not the first to say that, and you won't be the last." She bit into her hot dog. What was it about hot dogs? Sometimes they just hit the spot—the perfect lunch, but they were so bad for you. She glanced at him. Kind of like men.

"Tell me about your list of suspects."

She explained walking the gauntlet. She avoided his gaze

while she spoke, but it warmed her as much as the sun on her face.

When she chanced to glance at him, his gaze traveled along her face, her throat, her hair, his scrutiny carrying a tenderness that made her heart do a tap dance. She tried to ignore it and concentrate on her words. As she finished recounting suspects, she turned to him.

If she reached up, she could caress his face, run her fingers along his lips, so soft, so close. She breathed in the woodsy scent of his aftershave. Heat sparked in her gut and spread from there.

She met his gaze. He had been focused on her story, actually listening. This made him even more attractive. Now, apparently aware she was no longer speaking but looking, just looking at him, he blinked.

She turned away and coughed. "I need to get home."

"On a beautiful day like this? After a gourmet meal? Why not stick around a while?"

She could hear his dimpled grin. She was tempted, so tempted. But a little voice said, "Run." She stood, brushing hot dog bun crumbs off the front of her capris. She picked up his jacket and folded it, the woodsy scent faint.

"What about the police report? They could add it to the powder incident, start a paper trail." He stood beside her. "For what it's worth, I think you should report it."

"Report that someone put a mouse in my drink? They'd laugh me out of the station."

"But the note, Layla."

She handed him his jacket, and his hand lingered on hers, just for a heartbeat. Long enough to tell her she needed to get home *now*. "Thanks for lunch, Jack. You shouldn't have splurged though."

That laugh. Those crinkling eyes.

Go home.

"Next time I'll find a nicer restaurant far enough away that they'll be no batting women."

Part of her wanted to say, "I'd like that." That would be the normal response of any other sane woman. Instead, she said, "I don't think so." She turned to leave. She was afraid she'd change her mind.

"You don't let anyone in, do you?"

She halted. Slowly, she turned back to him. "What did you say?"

He approached her. She backed up a step. He was too close.

The peaceful azure sky behind him was a backdrop for the blue of his eyes, matching perfectly. But his gaze was not peaceful. His brows arced down, his usual smile gone.

"I said, you don't let anybody get close."

She raised her chin. "Yes, I do."

He cocked his head. "Who? Connie?"

The hot dog she'd just eaten did a somersault. "Mariana."

"Is she another one of your best friends?"

"We work together."

"And you hang out all the time?"

"We go to lunch ..." She couldn't bring herself to lie even more by adding "all the time."

His gaze bored into hers until she had to look away.

"Well, at least you go to lunch with somebody."

She glared at him.

"Look, I'm just trying to help."

"I don't need your help." She turned and stalked to her car.

FIFTEEN

Jack watched her leave. She didn't accentuate swaying her hips like most women did when they knew he was watching. Hell, he doubted she cared if he were watching. But her walk was sexier than any other woman he'd watched walk away ... and there'd been many.

Layla glided, her shoulders and back straight, saying, "Don't mess with me." Her long legs moved with grace, the high heels she wore creating a dizzying effect. He folded his jacket over his clasped hands and held it discreetly lest anyone be aware of his enjoyment of this view. She held her head high. Yes, she was right. She didn't need help. But he'd never wanted to help anyone so much in his life.

He glanced at the courthouse. The police station where his buddy, PJ, was a cop was nearby. Layla didn't have to know he was trying to help. And hadn't Clarence asked him to watch out for her? He had to keep his promise.

He slapped his forehead. *Damn, I didn't clear up that doctor confusion.* She pulled out of the parking lot and sped down Ionia

Avenue. Based on her response to his next lunch invitation, did it really matter?

SEVERAL COPS GREETED him as he passed through the lobby of the station. Phones jangled, a hooker sauntered toward him as she headed toward the exit, her pungent perfume almost knocking him over. She made eye contact and winked, and he shook his head.

A man who had clearly imbibed too much, swaying as he waved his arms to make his point, argued loudly with a detective. And behind the glass of the captain's office, his friend, Patrick James O'Keefe, was getting reamed out by his boss, Captain Reginald Winston. A typical day at the station.

Jack took a seat at PJ's desk, waiting for the tirade to finish. What rule did he break this time? PJ O'Keefe was a top undercover detective, though his methods were sometimes questioned by his superiors. But PJ did what he needed to do to bust criminals who preyed on innocent, vulnerable people ... even if it meant taking some liberties.

"I'm warning you, O'Keefe, you'd better toe the line!" Reggie Winston boomed. If Jack could hear it out here, he imagined PJ's ears were ringing. He scrolled through Instagram on his phone when a text message popped up.

Meredith: So good to see you the other night. Call me.

Things hadn't ended badly with her. They'd just faded out. He'd stopped calling, she'd stopped texting, they'd both moved on. Last he'd heard, she was dating a guy in finance. Maybe it didn't pay off.

The door to Reggie's office opened, and he fired a last volley at PJ as he exited. "I mean it this time, O'Keefe. Keep your nose clean."

PJ wiped his nose with his sleeve as he ambled toward his desk. He grinned at Jack.

"Hey, man. What's up?"

"What's up with you? That sounded like a Sunday thunder sermon."

PJ glanced back at Reggie's office. "Ah, that's Reggie's end-of-the-week rant. I was the target this time. I set up a sting with a punk drug ring, and it went south. It'll take some time to set something up again."

"I'm sure your plan was on the up-and-up." Jack laughed and slipped his phone into his jacket pocket.

"Always is." Though he was twenty-five, PJ's grin and youthful freckled face and auburn hair made him look like a leprechaun. At only five foot five, he could pass as a teen, though his stocky build deterred bullies who wanted a piece of him. And he'd been fighting schoolyard bullies since first grade, so martial arts and gym workouts were part of his daily routine. His scruffy, long hair and beard allowed him to infiltrate gangs and bust drug dealers.

"Of course," Jack said with mock seriousness.

PJ dropped into his chair, stretched, and cupped the back of his head in his hands. "As I was driving back here to the station for my spanking, I spotted you with some babe. Didn't look like Meredith."

Jack instinctively touched his pocket where his phone rested. He'd have to answer her text.

"No, not Meredith. Layla Forrester."

PJ frowned. "Forrester. Forrester. Why does that sound familiar?" He tilted his chair back and studied the ceiling as if the answer lay somewhere in the acoustic tiles. "Have you dated her before?"

"No, and I'm not dating her now."

"Wait a minute. Layla Forrester. The woman who had the suspicious powder threat? I saw that on the news."

"That's right. I was a first responder."

"She's pretty hot. Why aren't you dating her?"

Jack wondered that himself. Kind of. She was so strong, but she was so stubborn. So aloof, but also so tender with Clarence. She'd practically ordered him out of Clarence's room, she'd treated her best friend like crap, and she'd turned him down for another lunch date. Probably a moot point.

"She's nothing but trouble." He scrubbed his chin. "So how can I find out about the investigation into that?

"Into what? Forrester's case?" PJ thumped his chair to the floor and sat forward. "Uh-oh. You've got it bad. The last time you asked for this was when you were dating the drug lord's daughter. Granted, you didn't know her father was a drug lord, but you were going to be her knight in shining armor and rescue her. I found you unconscious behind a dumpster."

"Well, no worries here. Number one, I know her father and he's a great guy, and number two, she wants nothing to do with me."

"Playing hard to get, huh? Women. They have all these tricks they think we can't see through."

"No trick. She's an ice queen." He stared out the window. "But you know, she's not really.

PJ slapped him on the right shoulder.

Jack winced.

"Oh, yeah. Sorry, man." He patted his left shoulder. "But you've got it bad. Wanting to be her knight in shining armor and all."

Jack shot him a "what are you talking about?" glare.

"You know, the knight in shining armor comes to rescue the damsel in distress. Didn't your folks read you fairy tales when you were little?"

Jack snorted. "My father read me the racing form; does that count?" *Usually through blurry eyes after he'd passed out the night before.* He could hear his mother sniffling in the corner, pressing an ice bag to her blackened eye.

"Well, you're her knight."

Jack thought about her with her arms crossed, more pissed off than scared, when he'd entered her office. "She's no dame in distress. So, can you get me any info on the investigation?"

PJ grinned at him. "Sure, Sir Knight. I'll see what I can do. And it's damsel, not dame."

"Whatever. Thanks. See ya."

Holding his shoulder, Jack stretched his right arm out to the side and circled it around as he left the station. Nursery rhymes, hah. His life had been filled with an ogre, and now he wanted an ice queen. Maybe he was a knight. Or maybe he was a fool.

SIXTEEN

Sunday, May 17

Layla leaned toward the mirror, widening and examining her right eye. A broken blood vessel spread pink veins throughout her eyeball. Yesterday's work marathon had taken its toll. Her shoulders and neck ached from sitting at the kitchen table, poring through notes and court files. But she had gotten through a weekend's worth of work on Saturday, and today she was free to spend the afternoon with Dad.

Three years ago, she'd petitioned the city to build handicapped accessible ramps along the river so people in wheelchairs or who used walkers could enjoy the view close up. She'd demanded a fishing dock with a dedicated area for wheelchair anglers.

The first year it was built, she'd taken Dad fishing every weekend, but since her promotion, she increasingly spent weekends preparing for the upcoming week's court appearances. She would begin to remedy that today. Somehow, she would manage her caseload better and free up at least Sundays to spend with Dad.

She dabbed at her red eye. If this was the cost, so be it.

When she arrived at Brookside, she jogged to the door. She'd missed the familiar energy and excitement of a fishing excursion with Dad. *Geez, I've become a workaholic. But that changes today.*

Out of the corner of her eye, she caught a movement and turned. Standing beside her SUV, stood Dwayne. He yanked out the cigarette that dangled from the corner of his mouth and snorted. "I saw you at Spring Fest last weekend." His grin sickened her.

She approached him and growled, "Did you put that mouse in my drink?"

He laughed, then took a deep drag of his cigarette, blowing the smoke in her direction. "If I was gonna put something in your drink, lady, it wouldn't be a stupid mouse." He leaned toward her. "Somebody else must hate you, but not as much as I do." He dropped the butt, squishing it under his dirty boots. He turned and sauntered off.

He got in his car and sped away. When he was out of sight, she stood with her arms tightly crossed, unable to move. Was he lying? She couldn't tell. But he'd definitely jumped to the top of her list of suspects. Though with Trevor fresh out of jail, he had some competition there.

The week had been calm. No more threats, no lurking stalker. She'd put the threats out of her mind; the stalker was nothing but a coward. But Dwayne had brought all this back to her mind.

She took a few cleansing breaths. Let it go. This day was for Dad. Turning, she headed toward the entrance to Brookside, taking more cleansing breaths along the way.

After greeting the girl at the desk and signing in, she hurried to Dad's room.

Empty.

He's probably in the middle of a hot euchre game, but I'll make him an offer he can't refuse. She entered the game room. Residents occupied two tables, one with two ladies working on a jigsaw puzzle, the other with four men playing euchre.

One of the euchre players waved at her. "Hey, Layla. Looking for your father?"

"Yeah. Is he outside?" She inspected the French doors that led to a courtyard.

"No, he's on a fishing excursion at Riverside Park."

She raised her eyebrows. "Oh, that's nice. Thanks."

Of all the days for Brookside to offer a fishing trip, why today? All her plans to surprise him with time for just the two of them were down the drain. Well, she could at least go out there and join them since she had her fishing gear in the car. Come to think of it, she had Dad's fishing gear, too. No wonder Brookside was so expensive. They equipped residents with sports equipment for outings.

WHEN SHE REACHED the parking lot near the wheelchair accessible dock at Riverside Park, she didn't see the Brookside van. *Damn, I hope I didn't miss him.*

Since Dad must already have some kind of rod, she would leave his in the car. He was pretty particular though and had gone through many before he found what he called "the perfect rod." As an afterthought, she grabbed his anyway, just in case. Dad was laidback about everything except fly fishing—and cribbage. She'd also bring his vest. She smiled as she hefted his heavy vest with its array of gear and hand-fashioned ties out of the back of the SUV and closed the door. He'd never forgive her if she forgot to bring this.

Slinging her waders over her left arm, she carried their rods and their gear down toward the river. The temperature had settled in at a comfortable seventy-four degrees, and the sun added warmth on her back and neck. The earthy smells of the river and its muddy, marshy banks reached her, and she inhaled deeply. Just what she needed after her encounter with Dwayne.

Above her, an oriole trilled his clear, musical notes, and the serenity she always found by the water flowed through her. The blue effect. She could picture her blood pressure decreasing with each step. Why didn't she make a point to do this every weekend? *Because you need to hustle, and you know it.*

A breeze off the river welcomed her as she descended the wooden ramp and searched the dock for Dad. There he sat, talking to someone who was standing just below him in the river. Her heart felt light. Though she did not like surprises, Dad loved them. He'd be tickled that she showed up.

He laughed, the sound ringing across the water. She had eyes only for him. How she loved him. After Mom died, he'd spent every minute he could with her. Coached her softball team, never missed a game she played, never missed her forensic debates, escorted her down the aisle—both ways. Down the aisle, and then back up it. Past all the whispers. Past all the sympathetic eyes.

She shut that image out of her mind. She would not let it spoil her day.

"Hey, Dad, I was going to surprise you, but Brookside beat me to it."

"Hey, Sliver." He lifted his face to receive her kiss. She hugged him tightly. Even if her surprise was ruined, they were together. When she straightened, she scanned the dock, but she didn't see any Brookside people here. She shaded her eyes and looked back up the riverbank. No staff.

"Did the Brookside people just leave you here alone?"

"No, honey. Jack brought me!"

Her stomach plummeted. He may as well have said, "I don't love you anymore."

"What?" She looked toward the river where Jack stood in knee-deep water in waist-high waders. "Jack?" she squeaked. She was the child who didn't get invited to the birthday party. She swallowed against the lump in her throat. Her head swam as she tried to make sense of this scene.

Dad clamped his rod into the holder on the railing and took her hand. "Honey, you've been so busy, and we just decided the day was too beautiful to stay indoors and play cribbage."

A knife through her heart.

"I was going to surprise you today. I was going to bring you here. But ..." She shrank inside herself. Blood pounded in her ears so that, though Dad's lips moved, she couldn't hear what he said. Her face flamed and her body chilled. Familiar sensations she'd spent three years trying to forget. Now they consumed her.

Jack climbed up the bank. "Hi, Layla. Glad you can join us."

Join us? She ignored the sting of her fingernails digging into her palms. Her clenched fists kept her hands from shaking ... or punching. She stepped away from Dad.

"No, I'll leave you to your fishing." She wanted to throttle Jack. She wanted to throttle Dad.

Dad reached for her. "Please stay, Sliver. I didn't know you'd have today free. We would have called you."

We. We would have called you. Could this get any worse?

"No, really. I need to get back to work. I only thought ..." She grabbed the back of a bench until the dizziness passed. This couldn't be happening. All that had mattered was Dad; everyone else had left her. *But Dad won't leave you.* She looked at his frail body, a shell of the rugged man he had been. Yes, he would. Not right away, but sooner than she'd ever be ready for. She looked at Jack. In a way, Dad was leaving her right now.

"I'll see you tomorrow, Dad." She gave him a peck on the

cheek, then turned and jogged up the ramp, the waders crashing against her leg all the way up. Fool, fool, fool.

She pitched the fishing gear and waders into the back of her SUV and dropped her rod beside the pile on top of the specialized wheelchair lift. *Damn men.* Slamming the back closed, she hurried to the driver's door and scrambled in. Revving the engine, she pulled out, burning rubber on her way.

What more could Jack do to make her want him to disappear from her life?

CLARENCE'S GAZE never left his daughter as she disappeared up the bank and into the parking lot. Removing his bucket hat, he wiped his balding head with his handkerchief. He wiped at his eyes and took a deep breath.

Jack stood nearby, allowing him to regain his composure.

Birds carried on conversations in the trees above them, and a rowdy group of teens floated by on inner tubes. From the sound of their jollity, they were imbibing beer pilfered from their parents' refrigerators or purchased by an older sibling. They waved wildly.

"Hey man! Awe-*hic*-some day, huh-*hic*?" One boy called, attempting to stand and ending up in the water. Fortunately, his friends were still coordinated enough to pull him back onto his tube, heckling him the whole time.

At least they were happy drunks—unlike his father. Their slurred speech was all too familiar. Jack rubbed his right shoulder and flexed his arm.

Clarence continued to stare even though Layla had disappeared from view. "I didn't mean to hurt her."

Jack sat on the bench beside his wheelchair. "Of course you didn't. She knows that."

Clarence dragged his attention to Jack. "You don't understand, son. She's been hurt an awful lot. Lost her mother at age thirteen. I did the best I could, but some pain I couldn't take away."

Jack shivered.

"She's tough, but you see, she's had to be. That's what got her through the other times when she hurt so bad." He looked back at the stairs as if, just maybe, she'd return. "Deep in here," he poked his index finger at his chest, "she's kind. What's that word? Fragile. You know what I mean? People don't understand why she acts like she does. She's carrying hurt from a long time ago, and from not so long ago."

Jack nodded. "I understand."

Clarence grunted. "I thought you did." His shoulders slumped and he took his pole from the holder. "I don't think they're biting anymore. Let's head back."

"Sounds good. I'll pack up our stuff."

Fragile. Of all the words he would have used to describe Layla, fragile hadn't come to mind. Now Jack, too, looked back at the ramp. Hoping she'd return? He frowned. Trouble. That's the word he'd use to describe Ms. Layla Forrester.

SEVENTEEN

Monday, May 18

Jack didn't hate Monday mornings; he just wished they didn't come so fast. With the exception of running into Layla and feeling like he'd done something wrong in taking Clarence fishing, the weekend had been great. A good run and workout Saturday morning, errands in the afternoon, and a Guinness on the deck while he listened to the game. Not exactly a social butterfly, but sometimes after a week of emergency calls, he just wanted some peace and quiet.

Before he got in his truck, he checked his text messages. Another one from Meredith and one from PJ. He still hadn't replied to Meredith, but right now he wanted to hear from PJ in case he had news on the investigation. Since it was on his way, he'd swing by the station.

After all, he did promise Clarence that he'd watch out for her. Even though that was the last thing she wanted from him.

Traffic moved along smoothly, allowing his mind to wander. Recently, Layla's face came to mind when he wasn't focused, and she didn't fail him this morning.

Look, I didn't kidnap your father and force him to come fishing with me. He's a grown man, he can hang out with whoever he wants. I'm sorry if I hurt you. How can I make it better between us?

These arguments always ended with those two sentences. And for the life of him, he couldn't figure out why he would ever want it to be better between them. Except that she made his heart race as though he'd jumped rope for an hour. But she was so damn stubborn...and brave. He'd never met a woman who drove him this crazy. What had Clarence called her? Fragile? But sometimes she was so fierce.

"Fragile, my ass." He snorted as he pulled into the station.

PJ looked scruffier than usual this morning, wearing a dirty heavy metal band T-shirt under a plaid flannel shirt frayed along the buttonhole placket and cuffs. His jeans and work boots looked like a hard day after a demolition job. Thick stubble attested to the fact that he hadn't shaved. Getting within three feet of him confirmed that he hadn't showered.

"Got a hot date today?" Jack waved his hand in front of his face. "You're sure to score."

"I know you want me." PJ puckered his lips and made smacking noises.

"Like I want the clap. Got your text. What's up?"

PJ glanced toward Reggie's office. He was reaming someone else today. "That guy's blood pressure is going to explode out the top of his head." PJ rummaged through the messy files that littered his desk and recovered an envelope from the gas and electric company. Based on the mustard stain, he might have used it to cradle a hot dog from Dogs on Monroe.

"Here it is." Rolling his chair next to Jack's, he pointed to the chicken scratches scrawled across it. "Check it out, man."

Jack squinted at the random markings on the envelope.

Maybe one of them partially covered with mustard was a capital
H, but he wasn't sure. "Is this how you fill out reports?"

"No. I type them."

"Good thing. I can't read a word here. Is that an H?"

PJ looked at him like he was crazy. "That's an N. Can't you
read?"

"Not this. Interpret for me.'

PJ stole a glance toward Reggie's office and hunkered down
toward Jack. "The substance that was found in ... what's her
name again?" He flipped the envelope over, but all it revealed
was the return address of the gas and electric company.

"Layla." Just saying her name brought the image of her
standing on the dock, loaded down with fishing gear, smiling at
Clarence, her face soft with love and devotion for him. The way
the sun through the trees had dappled her hair, changing it from
dark brown to full of golden highlights. Then her face darkened.

He looked up. PJ stared at him.

"Man, you're in deep."

Jack straightened. "So, translate these hieroglyphics for me."

"Okay, so most of it was calcium citrate, like for a health
supplement. But here's the thing. Mixed in was a small amount of
fentanyl which is usually mixed with heroin, based on what's
showing up on the streets. Whoever sent this has connections to
local dealers, but he wasn't mixing it to sell on the street.
Whoever did this was sending a message. But for someone to lay
out some cash for the fentanyl, now you're talking about a twisted
mind. One that might not stop at a threat."

PJ's words hit him like ice water. Jack rubbed his eyes, partly to
erase the feeling, partly to hide his reaction from PJ. Steve was right;
he had a lousy poker face. When he opened his eyes, PJ had pulled his
chair back up to his desk, elbows resting on the disarray of files, and
was chewing on a number two pencil. To his credit, he said nothing.

"There's more, right?" Jack clasped his hands, his knuckles white, keeping his cool.

PJ swerved in his chair toward him. "I've infiltrated a gang that uses this mixture. It's been in the bigger cities for a while, but it's newer on the streets around here. As far as I know, this ring is the only one who's dipped into this pool, but it won't be long before the other gangs give them a run for their money." He leaned forward, elbows on knees, hands clasped. "The point I'm making here, Sir Knight, is that whoever sent this to her is connected to this gang as either a user or a dealer. Or the Big Man."

Jack whistled softly. "And whoever this is has been following her."

"What do you mean?"

Jack described the mouse in Layla's drink and the note.

"There should be video from the street cams," PJ said. "I'll see if I can pull it. But with the crowds during the festival, it'll be tough." He glanced at the captain's office.

"Thanks. That would be great." Jack pushed off the chair, but PJ placed a hand on his left shoulder and pushed him back down.

"She doesn't know, does she?"

"Know what?" Jack scratched his chin.

"That you're asking about all this."

"No." He shrugged.

"Or how you feel about her."

"Look, I'm just trying to help, okay?"

"Got it. Later dude." PJ winked and shredded his cryptic note.

As he left, Jack opened the door for an incoming elderly woman who cradled her shih tzu.

"Thank you, young man."

For as tiny as the dog was, it gave a mighty growl.

"You're welcome, Ma'am." Jack wished he wore a hat he could tip. *See? I just like to help people.* Just because he'd held the door for her didn't mean he wanted to sleep with her.

EIGHTEEN

Layla marched into Mariana's office. She couldn't live any longer with the lie she'd told Jack. He'd been right. She had no friends. Not anymore. Not since she shunned them all after Mark left her at the altar three years ago. She wasn't sure she knew how to have a friend anymore.

Mariana looked up in surprise.

"Get your purse; we're going to lunch." That was not what she had practiced. She squeezed her eyes shut. "Crap."

"With that kind of sweet talk, how can I resist?" Mariana's face was deadpan.

Layla nodded. "Sorry. Are you free for lunch?" She fought back a cough that threatened; it would sound like mockery.

"Yes. So, this is an invitation, not an order, right?" Mariana's dark eyes twinkled.

Layla flopped onto a chair. "I'm not so good at this."

Mariana patted her hand. "This is a good start. I'll get my purse."

LAYLA HAD THOUGHT about reporting the mouse and the threatening note, but she didn't want to give the threats credence. Still, the idea kept poking at her like an annoying gnat all day while she tried concentrating on her case file. Maybe Jack was right ... ugh, she hated even thinking that. But she probably should have reported it. She figured they had a record about the incident with the powder. It couldn't hurt to update that file.

When she entered her condo, she dropped her briefcase on the kitchen chair and picked up a tray with some of Miss Ida's dishes. It had been past eleven after she'd washed them. Too late to return them then. Should she take them to her before she made dinner? That might look like she was hoping for another meal. She set them down and pulled out a frozen dinner. A step up from Ramen noodles. There was one glass of moscato left in the bottle, so she sipped that while she cooked. She snorted. Cooked? While she microwaved stringy grilled chicken and soggy vegetables. She longed for pizza, but that was a weekend luxury.

When she'd finished cleaning up and was satisfied her stomach wouldn't growl, she headed across the hall with the tray to which she'd added a bag of Lindt chocolates. She was proud of herself that the bag was still sealed.

Miss Ida greeted her with a hug and a cry of delight at the chocolates. "Come on in. Isaiah's visiting. Let's open this up right now."

Miss Ida's son, Isaiah, rose from his seat, dwarfing the modest dining room table. Miss Ida's condo was larger than hers since it was a two-bedroom. She actually had a kitchen, but then Miss Ida deserved a kitchen. A true kitchen would be wasted on Layla.

Isaiah greeted her with a kiss on the cheek. She smiled up at him. "Hey, Isaiah. How's the crime in Grand Rapids these days?"

He hitched up his belt, jangling the handcuffs and Taser that hung from it and broke into a smile. Isaiah's smile never failed to lift her spirits. The corners of her mouth lifted in sync with his. No one could resist that pull.

"I'm doing my best to keep the streets safe, Layla."

This was their routine whenever they met. Until now, Layla thought of it as just that—a friendly routine. Now it didn't seem so lighthearted. She rubbed the goosebumps that had risen on her arms.

"You okay?" Isaiah's smile disappeared into a concerned frown. "You can't be cold. Mama always keeps her condo set above seventy degrees."

"You will, too, someday," Miss Ida said from behind her and then fell silent.

Layla felt Miss Ida's gaze boring into the back of her head. Like telepathy, in her mind she heard, "Tell him child, tell him." She glanced back to see if Miss Ida had actually spoken, but her lips were pressed together, her arms folded, her foot tapping. Oh yeah, she had sent a telepathic message all right.

Isaiah looked from her to his mother and back. "What's up?"

Layla looked back at Miss Ida, who raised her eyebrow and lowered her head like a mama bird about to nudge her fledgling out of the nest.

"Okay, okay." She flopped on a dining room chair, and Isaiah resumed his seat. "I've received two threatening notes."

"Two!" Miss Ida stood with her hands on her hips. "Why didn't you tell me?"

"Because I thought it was merely a poorly conceived prank. I didn't want to worry you." She turned back to Isaiah. "One at Spring Fest when a dead mouse ended up in my iced tea."

"Good Lord." Miss Ida scrunched up her face.

Layla nodded. "The first one was a letter that contained white powder."

If Isaiah'd had any hair, he'd be smoothing it back, but he kept his head shaved and shiny. He rubbed his head and let out a long sigh. "Thank you for telling me."

She gave him a sidelong glance. "You knew about the first one, didn't you?"

He looked at Miss Ida, then at her, and nodded. "The police report came through along with the analysis of the powder." He looked at Miss Ida again. "Sorry, Mama, I couldn't say anything without Layla's permission."

"I understand, son." Even with his admission of omission, her eyes shone with pride as she smiled at him.

"I couldn't say anything to you either, Layla. Privacy laws. So, I'm glad you told me. Detective Smythe noted that you didn't offer much help to the investigating officers though. How unusual." His eyes danced.

She rolled her eyes. "I had nothing to tell. I have no idea who did this ... these things. I still have no idea. At first, I suspected Seth Thomas, a colleague. He just happened to show up right after the mouse appeared."

"So, you two don't get along, I take it." Isaiah reached along the table, then detoured and reached for the steaming cup of coffee Miss Ida had just poured for him. Layla suspected he'd automatically reached for a pen to take a report and made a smooth move to the coffee mug instead.

"No, even when we got along, we didn't get along. We had a brief fling. It didn't end well. Then I got promoted over him, so he resents me." Layla looked up at Miss Ida as she set a cup of green tea in front of her and plate with Lindt chocolates between her and Isaiah. "Thank you." She turned back to him. "I mean, nobody at the office likes me much, except Mariana and Jimmy. Anyway—"

Isaiah held up his hand. "Jimmy who?"

She smiled. "Jimmy Hunter. He's a sweet young man who works in the mailroom."

"Going for younger men these days, are you?" Isaiah raised an eyebrow.

She chuckled. "Well, I do think Jimmy has a crush on me. I helped him get the job, but it was kind of a penance in a way. I also helped convict his brother on charges of drug dealing."

"And?"

"Jimmy is developmentally disabled. He has Down syndrome, and his brother, Trevor, basically raised him. Dad's an abusive bully who suffers with alcoholism. Tough situation. With Trevor incarcerated, helping Jimmy get into a group home kept him safe and allowed him to work. So, I helped him get hired at my firm." She stared at the table, tapping her spoon on the tablecloth.

"And ..." Isaiah tipped her chin up.

"And the other day Jimmy told me Trevor just got out of jail."

"For dealing drugs."

"Yes."

"Anyone else on your suspect list?" He gave her a half smile.

"There's a guy who worked at Brookside. He was fired because I reported him for bringing Dad the wrong meds. Dad could have become seriously ill, maybe even died, if we hadn't checked. His sister still works there. I've run into him a couple of times, and he's been pretty threatening."

Isaiah nodded, now his gaze glued to the table, and she suspected, memorizing every detail she said. "Why didn't you file a report?"

"That's what Jack said."

"Jack who?"

Miss Ida hummed, then clicked her tongue.

"That's Mama's matchmaking call. Did she fix you up with this guy?"

"No. He was my doctor in the hospital. And he's been stalking me ever since."

Isaiah sat bolt upright. "Stalking you?"

She shook her head and waved a hand in front of her face. "No. I'm kidding. Though he's stalking Dad."

Isaiah turned to his mother with a look of confusion. "Can you translate this for me?" He looked back at Layla. "You're usually very precise when you speak, but you've got me going around in circles here."

Miss Ida sat down at the head of the table like a referee between them. "This Dr. Jack is trying to help Layla. He nicely visited her father while she was kept overnight at the hospital. Now she feels like Jack stole her best friend away."

Miss Ida had strung her bow and shot the arrow of truth right through Layla's heart. She hunched a bit as if she'd been hit. "He takes Dad fishing ..."

"Once," Miss Ida interjected.

"And they play cribbage. ..."

"Once."

Layla shot her a look. "And now he's always there when I visit Dad."

"Mmm-hmm." Miss Ida folded her arms and sat back. "And truth be told, I think he's sweet on her."

Layla blew out a long puff of breath.

Isaiah laughed. This time, she didn't laugh with him. Miss Ida's words still stung too much.

Isaiah placed his hand on hers. "Come to the station tomorrow. I'll help you file a report. This could escalate into more serious threats ... or worse. He could try something again."

"But I had a professor who said if someone threatened you, they probably wouldn't harm you. They're chickenshit and would never confront you."

His deep brown eyes held hers, no trace of humor in them. "Layla, your professor is wrong. I see threats carried out every day. You need to take this seriously."

She nodded. Maybe she would feel better if there were a paper trail of the threats. "Okay. I'll stop by tomorrow."

"Good." He drained his coffee mug. "You're coming to my big bash Friday night, right?"

Now she smiled with him. "Wouldn't miss it."

"And you'll bring Mama along, right?"

"She's my date."

Miss Ida hummed a noise that was somewhere between Motown and disapproval. "We've got to find you something besides business suits to wear. You can't go celebrate when you're all trussed up tighter than a Thanksgiving turkey."

Layla tilted her head back and gazed at the swirls on the ceiling. She dreaded shopping—that was another reason she relied on her online discount and garage sale websites. No trying on, no waiting for a dressing room, no pawing through racks of clothing. Just point, click, pay. If it didn't fit, send it back. The only place she actually enjoyed shopping at was Monique's Unique Boutique. The name was corny, but Monique had a loyal clientele who apparently wore things only once and decided once was enough. Some items still had the tags attached. High end and hardly, if ever, worn.

But the main attraction was Monique, who was generous in both body and soul, and wore kaftans and head scarves and called everybody "honey." Layla was never offended by this because from Monique, the term of endearment was genuine.

"Yes, I'll wear something other than a suit."

"Something pretty, floral, flowing, romantic." Miss Ida's dreamy eyes focused on a distant memory. She refocused on Layla, dreamy eyes now stern. "Nothing tailored."

"I would do this only for you, you know."

Miss Ida's grin was ear to ear. "I know, child."

Layla stood. "I've got work to do." She kissed Miss Ida on the cheek and hugged Isaiah.

His deep voice stopped her in her tracks. "What time are you coming down to the station tomorrow?"

Her shoulders slumped. Busted. "Fine. I have a ten o'clock court appearance. How about nine?"

"See you then." He broke into a smile.

She smiled back. She couldn't help herself.

NINETEEN

Tuesday, May 19

Layla waited at the service counter for the desk sergeant to finish his call. She stared at the desk littered with memo pads, pens, pencils, and messages to be delivered. Whenever she was in a public place like the courthouse or the police station, she averted her gaze. She never knew when she might run into someone she'd gone up against as a prosecutor. Now that she was a defense attorney, it might be a defendant who didn't like how his or her case went down. And they usually blamed the attorney. Better to stare at memos and pens. Let them flip her off or swear at her back—Lord knew she was used to it.

A tap on her shoulder.

"Hey, Layla. Sorry to keep you waiting." Isaiah smiled at her. "I had to finish up with Captain Winston. He sometimes— scratch that—usually gets a little windy. C'mon in."

He led her into the main room of the station toward his desk at the far end. As they wended their way, a stocky man about five foot five meandered toward them. She guessed he was in his early twenties, maybe younger, and hadn't bathed in a week.

Her heart pounded. *This is what I picture my stalker looking like. Not someone I know. This guy is scary.* Eyeing his disheveled carrot-red hair, torn and wrinkled clothing, and heavy five o'clock shadow, she had no doubt he was a homeless man picked up for panhandling. So why wasn't he being escorted by a cop?

When he reached Isaiah, they slapped a high five.

"Hey, Isaiah," the man said.

"'Sup, PJ?"

"Heaven and the stock market. It's up 530 points today."

Layla clapped her mouth shut. A homeless man who followed the stock market? She balled her fists to keep from waving her hand in front of her face to ward off his odor.

"Layla, this is PJ O'Rourke. PJ, Layla Forrester."

PJ's jaw dropped. Then a glint of something in his eyes ... recognition? No, he looked like he was going to laugh. *Well, if you think I look strange, buddy, go find a mirror.* She stiffened and nodded. "How do you do?" Even to herself, she sounded curt.

PJ grinned like he'd just won the lotto. His teeth gleamed like a whitening toothpaste commercial. Apparently, he hadn't been homeless for very long.

He stuck out a hand. Was she supposed to shake it? Touch him? She recoiled and balled her fists tighter.

PJ threw his head back and laughed. "Later, man." He ambled off.

Isaiah's eyes sparkled. "Takes some time to get used to PJ."

"A bath would help."

"Here, sit down." He pulled a chair out beside his desk and she sat in it. Tapping on the keyboard, he woke his computer, hit a command and a form appeared on the screen. His fingers flew as he filled in the top portion. "Okay, now I'm going to take your statement about the second threat, then I'll merge it with the initial report of the first threat with the envelope."

She sat down and crossed her legs, swinging the top one back and forth. "It was just another prank. This guy is a coward."

He locked her gaze with his. "Layla, the first incident was serious. With the right combination of drugs in that powder, you could have been seriously injured, even killed. The second makes it clear he means business and he has access to you. You're a lawyer. Would you let a client decline to give evidence that might convict a criminal?"

His words made sense, but she had never been on this side of a crime. In the future, she'd be more sensitive to what her clients experienced.

"I thought the first incident was a prank. Taking me to the hospital seemed ridiculous—I felt fine." She took a deep breath. "This is all some kind of nonsense." She swept her arm out to indicate the whole department. Isaiah caught her wrist as it passed his face. He held it lightly and stared at her. She glared at him.

"Listen to me. I've seen bodies bleeding on the street of people who were threatened with far less. You need to take this seriously."

Though he spoke barely above a whisper, he commanded her attention. She jiggled her leg. She pulled her lips tight as Isaiah released his grasp. There was no sense arguing with him, so she didn't even try. The cacophony of voices, ringing phones, foot-steps, both hurried and reluctant, muddled her brain.

Isaiah's eyes softened. "Look, you're like my sister. Mama has made that very clear." He smiled. "I need to keep you safe or she'll kick my ass. Now, you don't want her to kick my ass, do you?"

He'd grounded her, and she released the breath she'd been holding. As usual with Isaiah, she couldn't help herself. She smiled. "She'd kick it good, too."

"I know she would!"

She sat back in the chair, closed her eyes, and related every detail she could remember of the recent incident, including seeing Dwayne and Crystal Brown nearby. Isaiah's typing kept pace with her account. When she finished, she opened her eyes and looked around at the people giving statements, being led in handcuffs, coming in for questioning, waiting to file personal protection orders. Like telepathy, their fears drifted to her along with the realization that she was them.

And she didn't want to be.

TWENTY

Dazed, Layla stared at a rack of dresses. She wanted to rush out of the store, run home, and lock herself in her condo. She turned toward the door, but a firm grip around her shoulders pointed her back to the rack.

Monique whispered close to her ear, "I believe you said you needed a dress, honey. Something feminine, something flowing and floral."

Layla rolled her eyes at her. "I was hallucinating. I was possessed. I didn't know what I was saying." She checked her watch. "I'll come back later. Urgent appointment."

The grip on her shoulders tightened. "Listen, Miss Priss, you are not going to deny me a sale. And you are especially not going to deny me seeing what you'd look like in one of these dresses." She released her grip. "You're not going to run now, are you?"

Layla slumped her shoulders and tilted back her head. "No, I won't run."

"Promise? Cross your heart?"

She swiped her right hand in an X across her chest then raised her hand. "Cross my heart."

Monique's hands flew as she slid dresses along the rack. "Wrong color, wrong size, wrong cut ..." Her mantra continued as she perused the options, occasionally lifting one and slinging it over her free arm. When she was satisfied, she steered Layla to a dressing room, hanging the selections on a hook. "I want to see every one of these on your body." She drilled her gaze into Layla. Like Miss Ida's place, this boutique allowed none of Layla's high-powered behavior. At work, she ruled with unchallenged authority, but here she reverted to her obedient school days. In a way, she was relieved.

Slipping on a floral print organza, she checked the mirror and almost vomited. She looked like Little Miss Muffet. She unzipped it.

"I heard the zipper. You'd better not be thinking of taking that dress off until I see it," Monique's warning sailed through the dressing room curtain.

"It looks ridiculous on me."

"Bring it."

Layla stepped out of the dressing room and stood in front of the three-way mirror. Two shoppers looked at her, then quickly returned their attention to the dress they had stopped at. Layla wanted to sink into the ground.

Monique inspected her. "Mmm-hmm. You're right. That's not working for you."

"No kidding."

"Attitude, Miss Priss," Monique scolded as she unzipped the dress.

At least the next dress didn't feel like she was a gardenia in her grandmother's living room drapes. Actually, she liked this black sheath dress with a bateau neckline and three-quarter sleeves. The two gathers at the waist made a nice silhouette without being clingy. This was the one. She stepped out.

The two shoppers looked up, nodded, smiled, and resumed shopping.

Monique folded her arms across her ample bosom. "Girl, you are not getting that dress."

"But I like it. Look how it fits." She turned with her back to the mirror and looked over her shoulder.

"It's black. It's modest. It's sensible. What I heard you say when you came in was none of those things."

"I was quoting Miss Ida. I don't want a fluffy, floral dress. You know that's not me, and I would feel foolish the whole night at Isaiah's party."

"But you need to branch out, explore, experiment." She eyed the floral hanging in the dressing room. "Okay, maybe I pushed you too far, but," she nodded toward the offending dress, "it ticked all the boxes you asked for."

Layla glanced at it, then quickly back at the mirror. "Yeah, I guess it did. Can it go away now?"

Monique took the dress and examined the sheath Layla had on. "Buy that one—it looks great. But not for the party. You gotta up your game."

Layla returned to the dressing room and whipped the curtain closed. "Damn dresses. Just let me wear one of my suits," she muttered.

"I can hear you, you know." Monique's reprimand breezed to her.

Layla loved the coral color of the next dress, and the material was soft and silky. Slipping into it, she stood and stared at her image in the mirror. Her complexion glowed, and the coral accentuated her brown eyes. The dress hugged her figure, highlighting all her curves with just enough décolletage showing. *My God, it shows every curve! But, damn, I look good!*

"Got that coral number on yet? Get it out here." Was Monique tapping her foot?

Layla pushed the curtain aside just enough to poke her head out. "I think it's too small."

"It's not too small. I've been fitting you long enough to know it's not too small. Now get out here and show me." Monique tugged the curtain aside.

The two shoppers gasped in unison and stared.

"Oh my gosh," one said, "I wish I could wear that dress and look like that."

Layla glared at her, and she turned away.

Standing in front of the mirror, she couldn't believe her eyes. She'd transformed into someone she didn't recognize.

Monique's husband appeared from the office. "Here are the sale tags you wanted." He stopped in his tracks and looked at Layla. "You need to buy that dress, Layla." He handed the tags to Monique, glanced again at Layla, then he returned to the office.

Monique cocked her head and raised her eyebrows. "Honey, you do."

Layla checked herself in the mirror, turning in each direction. *Even my butt looks good in this dress.*

"Take it off and I'll ring it up before you change your mind." Monique unzipped her.

Layla took the coral and the black dress to the counter. *If I chicken out, I can always wear the black.*

Monique gave her the stink eye. "I think you only need one dress for Isaiah's party."

"I know. But this will be my little black dress."

Monique placed only the coral dress in the garment bag.

"What are you doing? I don't need two bags"

Monique hung the black dress on the rack behind the counter. "This one needs to be pressed, and I noticed the hem needs some repair. You can pick it up Monday."

"Monique ..." Layla frowned.

"Sorry, we never let merchandise out of our store unless it's ready to wear that moment." She balled the hem of the skirt in her hands, causing wrinkles to form. She shrugged her shoulders and raised her hands, palms up. "See? It needs to be pressed, and I happen to know you don't own an iron."

Layla laughed. "You read my mind, didn't you?"

"Uh-huh. Girl, you're wearing that coral dress Friday night."

"You're impossible." Layla chuckled as she placed her credit card in the reader.

"Not yet. You need accessories. And lingerie." Monique flashed a wicked smile.

She had miles to go before she paid.

When she finally left the shop, burdened with shoes, a wrap, lingerie, plus jewelry and a purse for each dress, she had a comforting thought. *No one at this party will know me except Miss Ida and Isaiah anyway.*

TWENTY-ONE

Layla fumbled with her packages, trying to hit the button on her key fob to unlock the car. One small package slipped down along her thigh, hit her foot, and fell to the pavement.

"Damn." She bent to retrieve it, dropping another parcel.

"Can I help?"

Her heart did a somersault. She contemplated remaining in her bent position, hoping he'd go away. But since he was standing behind her and she was bent over, a passerby might misconstrue the encounter and she'd lose her job.

But do I want to stand up and face this guy?

She straightened and turned, caught by his eyes, the deep blue of a quiet ocean. Eyes that drew her in and made her draw a breath, a deep breath. Eyes that always held a hint of humor. Kind eyes that smiled even when she was rude or, at the very least, aloof.

"Hello, Jack." She struggled to sound detached.

"Hello, Layla." He shifted the grocery bag he carried and reached to help with the packages, but she held them tighter. He backed off. "Looks like you've been busy."

"Why are you here?"

He had the decency to erase his grin. "I'm on a shopping errand, too." He eyed her packages. "I hope I can be half as successful as you've been." He bowed and turned to leave.

She relented. "I'm sorry."

He turned and frowned. "For what?"

Another parcel slipped from her grip and landed at her feet.

He looked at it but didn't move to help. Then he raised his gaze to her, twitching his lips to the side, raising his eyebrows.

She bent to retrieve it and lost her grip on all the bags. "Damn."

He bowed reverently. "I would be most happy to help if you so wish."

She nodded. She hit the button on her key fob, and the rear hatch door glided up.

They both leaned down at the same time to pick up the parcels and bumped heads.

"Ow!" Jack rubbed his forehead.

"Damn!" Layla did the same.

"That seems to be your word of the day." Jack squatted down and picked up two bags.

Layla knelt beside him, gathering the smaller parcels. When she looked up, her gaze dropped from his eyes to his lips, curved in a soft smile, dimples setting it off in irresistible parentheses. Lips close enough to kiss.

He leaned forward and kissed her forehead where they'd collided.

She gasped.

"I thought it might help your owie." His eyes danced.

Rattled, she stood quickly, almost dropping the bags she'd recovered. He followed her to the back of the car and stowed the bags he carried beside hers. After he did so, he lightly placed his hand on the small of her back. She froze.

"Come have coffee with me." He spoke softly, hypnotically.

She wanted to agree. Her heart raced. "I ... I need to go. I need to get home." *You don't need to go anywhere. Stay.*

But he was the riskiest person in her life. She couldn't give in.

She didn't dare look at him again. She had only so much fight within her. She hadn't seen him for a week, but that didn't mean she hadn't thought of him. Often. Hadn't wished he'd be there when she visited Dad. And if she were honest with herself, that she hadn't missed him. But she didn't want to put her heart in danger again. And he, unlike Seth, was danger.

"Thanks for your help." She pressed the button to lower the back door. When it closed, she noticed how the car tilted to one side. She stepped into the street and stopped.

"Damn."

"And tomorrow's word will be *shit*," Jack said as he stepped off the curb to join her. "Oh, shit."

Her SUV leaned toward the middle of the street settling on two flat tires. A note fluttered, impaled on one tire with the ice pick that had been used to pierce both of them.

Her face and neck cooled as the blood drained from them. An ocean swished in her ears, drowning out the familiar sounds that had surrounded her minutes ago: traffic, conversations, music thrumming from low-riders, the natural rhythm of city life.

Jack tore a piece off his paper grocery bag and wrapped it around the pick, pulling it out of the flat tire. The note floated to the pavement, face up. He scanned the note and moved so she could read it.

I can see you right now.

Her head snapped up, and she scanned the street. She didn't recognize anyone. Storefront windows loomed, but the angle of the sun glared off the glass, concealing anyone in the coffee shop, bakery, nail salon, or any other store along the street. She turned to study the windows behind her, so close.

No one leered out at her from the grocery store, the physical therapy clinic, or the boutique. *Did that curtain fall at the second story window?*

"Layla."

She jumped at the sound of her name.

"Layla, let me take you to the police station. You need to report this."

She looked up at him, trying to comprehend his words, but the ocean swished louder. She scanned the street and store windows again. *People are going about their business as if nothing unusual had occurred. As if no one were threatening me.*

Jack placed his hands on her shoulders. She met his gaze. No longer did his eyes dance with humor or crinkle at the corners. Now the blue was dark with concern.

"Are you okay?"

He pulled her into his arms. She struggled against this refuge; someone was watching. She couldn't look afraid. This embrace had to mean something besides fear. *Think, Layla, think.*

You think this will rattle me, you punk? Watch this.

Steeling herself, she placed her hands along Jack's jawline, leaned in, and kissed him, long and full.

She risked a quick peek. Jack's eyes were open in shock. *Close your eyes. Close your eyes.* She leaned against him. As if hearing her, he slowly closed his eyes and wrapped her in his arms. His lips were warm and welcoming, his arms tight, holding her secure. She didn't want to pull away; she wanted more. And based on how Jack's lips were moving over hers, so did he.

She pulled back, but she remained in his embrace. "Check the windows. Is anyone watching us?"

He stifled a chuckle. "Lots of people are watching us. Was that your intent?"

She rested her arms on his chest. "I'm showing him that he can't get to me."

"And I thought it was my animal magnetism and irresistible charm at work."

She flicked her gaze to his face. "Wipe that damn smirk off your face, Jack."

"There's your favorite word again."

He silenced her ready retort, covering her mouth with his. This time her eyes bulged. But slowly, languidly, they closed. *Did I just moan? Oh God, no. I just moaned.* She pulled away and fumbled with the knot of hair at the nape of her neck. She cleared her throat. *Maybe he didn't notice that I moaned.*

"Well, that ought to do it. I don't think I looked frightened at all." She patted her hair again and tucked a strand behind her ear.

Jack's enigmatic expression shook her. "I sure hope he really is still around to see how not shook up you are. I mean, all that kissing for nothing. What a waste." Jack stroked his jawline as if pondering a deep mystery. "You'd better call a tow truck, and then I'll take you to the police station. Do you have any tweezers in your bag?"

"Tweezers? No." He certainly was unpredictable.

"We need something to pick up this note."

She opened the back door, leaned over the seat, and fished through the hatchback. "I have a hemostat on my fishing vest. That should work." She handed him the scissor-like instrument that curved into a blunt end.

He looked at the hemostat, then at her, and grinned. "You're quite resourceful." He gingerly picked up the note by one corner. "Open your purse."

She held her purse open, and he dropped the note in it.

"Let's get those packages loaded into my truck."

"What?" He had to be kidding.

"You can't drive this—two flat tires."

"I can call an Uber."

He stared at her. "Yes, I guess you can, but won't that look strange to your stalker who is watching us right now? I mean, that kiss you laid on me wasn't an 'I'll take an Uber' kiss."

She pulled her sweater tighter and looked around. "Okay. You're right." She opened the back of her car and pulled out packages. Jack stood beside her and grabbed several.

"Where's your truck?"

He nodded to the block ahead. "Just up there. We can load it up and drive around the block and park. Now don't get your hopes up; I don't mean to watch the submarine races ..."

She cocked her head and tapped her foot.

"I mean to see if anyone comes sniffing around your car before the tow truck gets here."

That made sense, though she hated to admit it. "Okay."

When they reached his truck, he opened the crew cab door to place the bags on the back seat. As he did so, one bag tumbled, spilling a silk chemise across the seat. The champagne fabric shouted against the black leather interior.

A funny choking sound came from Jack's throat, but he recovered. "My truck is honored." He made a mock bow.

"Stuff it, Doctor."

"About that ..."

But she was already around the side of the truck pulling open the passenger door.

He climbed into the driver's seat and put the key in the ignition. "Layla, you need to know that I'm not—"

She grabbed his hand. "Jack—look at that guy in the hoodie hurrying around the corner. I think he was watching us."

Jack tried to pull out, but a line of cars passed. When the street was clear, he eased out, drove to the end of the block, and turned the corner. He rolled down the street, and they searched both sides, but to no avail. The guy was nowhere in sight. Jack circled the block, and they tried to see into storefront windows, but the east side reflected the sun and the west side was solid concrete wall except for the entrance to a business.

Layla flopped back against the seat. She rested her elbow on the doorframe and rubbed her forehead. Why would some random guy be threatening her? It must be someone familiar or someone she worked with. Someone like Seth Thomas. Roland? Angela? Then again, there was Trevor, newly sprung from prison. And Dwayne, who seemed to be showing up a lot lately. Line 'em up.

"So, are you ready to go to the police station?" Despite her litany of suspects, Jack's presence soothed her. She shrugged the shoulder closest to him to block the effect.

"No. I'll call a tow truck and wait for them to arrive. They can take me home."

"I'll wait with you. You can stay in my truck."

"No."

"So, you'd rather be exposed out on the street with this guy hanging around than in the truck with me? That's not the message you sent a few minutes ago."

"The message I sent was not for you. It was for him."

"Oh, so you used me, did you?" Jack's mouth quirked up.

Raising her chin, she shifted in her seat and stared out the front window. "Noooo ..." She rubbed her chin. "Well, maybe." She stole a glance at him. *Damn eyes.* "Look, maybe I did, but I was trying to stay safe."

"I'd say you owe me for my part in your attempt to stay safe. Dinner at least. I don't think coffee is enough to make up for a 'passionate kiss to save my life.'"

She rolled her eyes. "I thought you had shopping to do."

He waved his hands toward the stores. The shops are closing, and tomorrow is another day."

When the tow truck pulled up and parked in front of her SUV, she hurried to it and showed the driver her tires.

The man whistled, then looked at her like she was a lake trout standing there. "You didn't drive the wrong way over a security grate, right?"

"Right."

"Uh-huh." He whistled again.

After they made arrangements to tow it to a garage, he pulled away, her SUV yanked up on the tow chain. A sigh escaped her lips before she could stop it.

"Okay, first to the police station, then to dinner."

"No, Jack." She turned to him. "I've already filed a report. What are the police going to do? Follow me around and see what he does next?"

"Well, for one, they could examine this pick and note for fingerprints."

She gave him a withering look. "Do you seriously think this guy wouldn't wear gloves?"

"There could be other clues on it. You need to—"

"I'm not going to the police with this."

His face darkened and he took a deep breath. "Dinner, it is."

She dropped her head back and looked at the trees swaying above her. "Okay, fine. Where are we going?"

"First I have to stop at home and put my frozen dinners in the freezer. I'm right around the corner from your dad, so let's stop in and see him. Then I'll take you to a little place I know."

How could she go with him?

How could she not?

JACK WANTED to take her hand. Wanted to assure her that everything would be okay. But he wasn't sure it would be. Whoever was stalking her was getting bolder, the threats growing. His promise to Clarence had sounded simple enough, but how could he watch out for her when she wouldn't watch out for herself?

He glanced at her.

She sat ramrod straight in the passenger seat, hands clasped in her lap, staring out the side window. She was scared, but she was trying to look so calm. Just like in her office with the powder.

"Why won't you go to the police with this?" He checked the rearview mirror. Now he was getting edgy. What if that guy followed them?

She shrugged. "I don't need to."

"Don't need to? This is the third time this guy has threatened you. At least add to your complaint so there's a paper trail. If you figure out who he is, you can get a personal protection order."

She continued to stare out the window.

"You think if you ignore him, he'll go away, don't you?"

Her lips tightened. *Bingo.*

"He won't go away, Layla. He's after you for some reason, and he won't stop until ..." Until what? He hurt her? Or worse? He stole another glance. Without thinking, he did reach and cover her hands. "Layla, I'm worried about you."

She stiffened and pulled away her hands. He might as well have said, "Layla, I'm a rattlesnake," based on her reaction. He put his hand back on the steering wheel. *Have it your way. You're on your own. I'll back off.*

Sure you will.

TWENTY-TWO

Jack's condo was on a shady city street less than a mile from Brookside. In fact, the pharmacy where she picked up Dad's prescriptions and personal care items was at the end of his block on Fulton.

He pulled into a driveway beside a huge red maple that shaded his front windows.

"Would you like to come in?"

"No."

He fought a smile. "Okay. Just give me a minute to stow my gourmet meals for the week."

She nodded, staring out the front windshield. But her eyes followed him as he jogged up the steps to his front door and let himself in. She twisted and studied the street they'd just driven down. All was quiet. She turned and checked the other direction. Same.

Was this what her life would be like from now on? Always waiting for someone to come out of the shadows? Wondering who was watching her? Lurking—where? Everywhere. That's what it felt like. She rubbed her arms though she wasn't chilly. She stared down the street.

When Jack opened the door, she jumped. Before climbing in, he did a quick scan of the street. His lips were pulled taut, his brows drawn down, but when he looked at her, he smiled, and his eyes softened.

Don't pity me. Don't care about me. It never ends well. She lifted her chin.

"Took you long enough."

He chuckled. "Oh, you missed me? That's the nicest thing you've said to me today."

She rolled her eyes. He was impossible.

CLARENCE BEAMED when Layla entered followed by Jack.

"It's nice to see you two finally made up." He laughed, then winked at Jack when Layla bent to hug and kiss him.

The minute they'd entered his place, his face broke into a grin at the sight of his daughter. They chatted comfortably, a relationship built on a lifetime of love and trust. Her eyes lit up when she looked at him, crinkling at the corners with laughter, alight with love.

Would he ever belong somewhere with devotion this deep?

"You okay, Sliver?" Concern shaded the love in Clarence's eyes.

Layla gave her father a brilliant smile. "You know me too well, Dad."

Jack smiled. She would tell him. Clarence would advise her. All would be well.

"As a matter fact, I had some car trouble with the car today. Jack was there and rescued me." Her smile remained brilliant, but in the split second it took her gaze to move away from

Clarence and burn into him, her eyes changed from loving to "I dare you to say something."

He opened his mouth, but she turned back to her father too quickly.

"I had it towed to the shop. It should be fixed in no time."

Clarence's shrewd eyes shifted to each of them.

He knows she's hiding something. Call her out, Clarence. Call her out.

"You should trade that heap in for a Lexus. You don't need to keep it to haul me around."

"What? I love that car. I don't want to give it up."

To keep from calling her out himself, Jack examined Clarence's rooms as if for the first time. The countertops in the small kitchenette were granite, the cupboards custom-built cherry. The light fixtures, the windows, even the furniture, were top quality. Brookside Manor was one of the top assisted living homes in the city. Certainly not cheap. He remembered Layla's office the day he'd gone in to rescue her. A corner office, expensive mahogany furniture, big law firm. Why wasn't she driving a Lexus? Or a BMW? Or a Porsche? Not a second-hand brown SUV. He scanned the room again.

"Right, Jack?"

His attention snapped back to her. "What?"

"The tow truck guy said it was an easy fix, didn't he?" Her eyes bulged at him and she inclined her head. He could almost hear her saying, "The only answer is 'yes.'"

"Yes. Yes. Easy fix."

"Hmph." Now Clarence was frowning at him as if he'd been disloyal.

Geez. I can't win here.

"How about fishing Saturday morning? I'll pick you up at six." Layla's smile never wavered.

Clarence reached out and covered her hand with his. Instead of pulling away, she turned her hand up and clasped his.

"You're so good to me, Layla."

She kissed his cheek. "I learned from the best."

"Will you be joining us, Jack?"

Her smile faded.

"Uh, I don't think so ..."

"Come on. It will be fun." The gleam in his eye told Jack that Clarence was having fun that very minute.

"No, Dad. Jack said no. Maybe another time." She kissed her father on the cheek, then turned to Jack.. "Let's go."

She pushed Jack out the door with barely enough time for him to bid Clarence good-bye. But not too soon to hear the man's chuckle.

As she hurried him along the corridor, she bumped into an aide who'd just stepped out of a room. The tray she carried crashed to the floor, spilling leftover mashed potatoes and peas on the shiny linoleum.

"Crap! Watch where you're going!" The aide spun around, and Jack recognized her as the woman who'd come into Clarence's room the other day. The one who was at Spring Fest with her brother, Dwayne. Her eyes grew large as she and Layla faced each other.

"Perhaps you should watch where you're going, Crystal." Layla's growl held no whisky-smooth notes.

Crystal's mouth pulled down into a sneer. "Sorry, Ms. Forrester." She spit the apology. "Looks like when you're around everything goes to hell."

They stared at each other.

"I'm sorry. I should have been more careful. Serious accidents happen when people aren't careful." Layla's tone was low and threatening.

Crystal smirked. "Yes, we should all be more careful, shouldn't we, Ms. Forrester?" Her eyes gleamed.

Again, they stared at each other in silence. Finally, Crystal bent to pick up the tray.

Layla took Jack's arm and continued down the corridor. Her grip threatened to stop his blood flow.

"Perfect flipping ending to a perfect flipping day," she growled.

"She's the one ..."

"Whose brother Dwayne almost killed my father with the wrong meds. Yes."

Jack looked back. Crystal scowled at them.

"You need to be careful," he warned.

She nodded. "I see that."

TWENTY-THREE

"Please take me home." Layla stared ahead through the windshield.

Jack turned on the engine. "Oh no. You still owe me a dinner, remember?"

She looked down at her hands clasped in her lap. "Jack, I apologize for kissing you earlier. It wasn't right for me to use you like that." She spoke softly, her whiskey-smooth voice barely above a whisper.

He fought back the smart-ass retort on the tip of his tongue. This was not easy for her.

"No problem. I get it." He started the engine but sat still for a moment. "Layla, I'd like to help however I can." And he knew it wasn't just because of the promise he'd made to her father.

Jesus. The deep desire he'd felt earlier thrummed through him again. He wanted to pull her into his arms and kiss her the way she'd kissed him, only he'd mean it. He gripped the wheel, resisting the urge to do exactly what would push her away more.

"Please take me home." The muscle in her jaw twitched, her fists balled—ready to slug him? Or holding herself back from feelings as deep as his own? Because for all her aloofness, sometimes when she looked at him, he saw interest, maybe even caring.

"Okay." He put his truck in drive and eased out of the Brookside Manor parking lot. A gentle rain pattered on the roof as they drove in silence. Jack hit a button on his screen and smooth jazz played soft and low. Jazz, Layla and her sultry voice, and a soft patter of rain. All of this soothed him as he navigated the streets, following her directions. She didn't live far from him or from Clarence, which didn't surprise him at all.

What did surprise him was the tidy neighborhood of modest houses and brick apartment buildings just a few miles from downtown. With her position at the law office, he'd expected an expensive condo in city center. She pointed out her parking spot and he pulled in.

"Thank you. I'm ... thank you." She got out of the passenger door and opened the back door to retrieve her packages.

Jack shut off the engine.

She froze. "What are you doing?"

"You'll need help getting all your packages in."

"I'm perfectly capable of handling my own bags." Rain spattered her hair as she stood there, arms akimbo, defiant and beautiful.

He stifled a grin. "You weren't downtown."

To prove her statement, she gathered all the bags and slammed the door. Two packages slid to the wet grass. When she bent to retrieve them, she lost three more. She jockeyed the rest.

Jack jumped out of the truck and scooped up the three bags and grabbed the other two by the cord handles. Then they sprinted to the front door. The snug foyer left little room for them, with all the bags, to maneuver the door closed. She tucked behind the door, but when she pushed it closed, it hit Jack in the shoulder, pushing him into her. She was up against the wall, the bags crushed between them.

"Leave them here. I'll come back down for them." She avoided his eyes and stared at his chin as she spoke. She smelled of flowers and fresh rain.

Jack held his place, close to her, close enough to feel her breath on his face. "What are you afraid of, Layla?"

She stiffened. "What the hell do you mean? I'm not afraid of anything. Certainly not you."

"Prove it." He spoke softly, an invitation rather than a challenge. He wanted her to trust him.

She met his gaze and raised one eyebrow. "What do you mean?"

"Prove that you're not afraid of me. Let me carry your packages up to your apartment. Let me stay for a drink. If you don't, I'll call you a lily-livered chicken."

He saw it—just for a second. A spark of humor in her eyes. He counted it a great victory.

"All right. You may carry my packages to my apartment. You may stay for one quick drink. One, Dr. Trenton."

"Please don't call me that."

"Why not?"

He didn't want to spoil this moment. This one moment where she opened just a crack to him. This moment where they stood so close her breath skimmed his chin. This moment where her eyes were smiling, and her silken voice made his knees weak.

"That you, Layla?"

A woman called down the stairs.

"Yes, Miss Ida." Layla answered, but her gaze did not leave his.

"You okay, child?"

The spell was broken.

"Yes. On my way up."

Jack pushed the door closed and followed her up the stairs.

"You're soaking wet! I made some soup—oh." Miss Ida caught sight of Jack. "Oh." Her voice rose an octave.

"Miss Ida, may I present Dr. Jack Trenton. He took care of me in the hospital."

"No—I'm not ..." Jack protested, but Miss Ida spoke over him.

"I have enough soup for two. And some fresh baked sourdough bread. I'll go get it and then I'll make myself scarce." She winked at Jack.

"But I'm not ..."

She had already closed the door to her apartment. Layla was unlocking hers. She ushered him in.

He studied the minimalist décor. Tasteful but not extravagant. A few pieces of art—an eclectic mix of modern and impressionist. The living area was cozy and inviting. A large, round antique clock hung between the two front windows. The sofa looked new, but the leather recliner spoke of many nights of use beside the reading lamp.

Layla headed to her bedroom and dropped her packages on her bed. Jack didn't dare enter. One, he didn't want her to mistrust him. Two, he didn't trust himself.

He handed her the rest of the packages, and she placed them on the bed and closed the bedroom door firmly. But not before he glimpsed the cream duvet and pillows that would lure anyone in. And an exotic Gauguin print above the headboard. Maybe Layla did have a wild side. He shook his head to erase his mind's meanderings.

"Red or white?" Layla brought out two bottles of wine.

"Red pairs well with soup."

She arched her eyebrow at him. He was beginning to like that. She tugged at the cork.

"I agreed to a drink, not dinner."

He crossed the few steps to the kitchen area. "Need help?" He reached for the bottle, but she wouldn't release it. Their hands met, wrapped around the cabernet sauvignon. She stopped struggling but didn't let go.

He let his hand slip down to cover hers, caressing her fingers. She didn't pull away. With his other hand, he brushed damp ringlets off her cheek.

She took a deep breath. She was giving a lot at that moment. She was allowing him in—maybe just a crack in the door. But in. He didn't want to blow it, though he desperately wanted to kiss her.

She let go of the bottle and reached for two glasses. When she turned back to him, her eyes, smoky with desire, met his straight on. He stepped toward her, leaning in, and she tilted her face to his, lips almost touching ...

A loud knock and they broke apart.

The door opened, and Miss Ida breezed in with a tray laden with a soup tureen and a napkin-lined basket filled with steaming sliced bread. If she noticed that she'd interrupted a romantic moment, she didn't give a clue. She bustled into the kitchen, set the tray on the table, gave Layla a hug, and breezed out, "I'll talk to you later, child," floating behind her.

Jack grinned at Layla and was rewarded with a half-smile. It was something. No, for her, it was a lot. "Well, I guess you're stuck with me for dinner after all." He waited.

After a beat, she pulled out two placemats from under the salt, pepper, and napkin holder on one side of the kitchen table and placed them opposite each other. Giving him a sidelong glance, she reached for two bowls, two spoons, and two plates, setting them on the placemats. Every movement was intentional, as if she were arguing with herself about whether or not she should complete each task. As if each were a step toward an end she wasn't sure she wanted to achieve. Or was she trying to seduce him? He hoped for the latter.

"I wish I had a Miss Ida neighbor." Jack poured wine into their glasses.

Layla smiled softly. "She's a gem." She ladled soup into their bowls.

He stretched and set the bottle on the counter since it was close enough, and there wasn't enough room for it on the table.

"Does she always bring you food?" He blew on the spoonful before he tasted it. He closed his eyes. "Oh my God, this is delicious."

Layla chuckled. "I have to suffer with her cooking quite often." She met his gaze and didn't look away this time.

The table was small enough that their legs bumped together when either of them moved. His leg rested against hers, and she didn't move away. The warmth seeped through his pantleg and forced him to concentrate on the soup.

She rose to get the wine bottle from the counter, and he stood beside her. She held the bottle, staring at it. He breathed in the scent of her hair, his eyes tracing her profile. Slowly, he placed a hand on her shoulder, and she turned to him. Her smoky gaze burned into his, then dropped to his lips.

She didn't look conflicted now.

He wrapped her in his arms and once more their faces were inches apart. Her breath was soft, and he pulled her close and pressed his lips to hers. She returned his kiss eagerly, parting her lips, inviting him in. Her arms slid up to his shoulders and pulled him closer. Her hips were against the counter, and as their embrace intensified, he pressed against her body, intoxicated with desire.

She moaned, a soft sound deep in her throat, but with the impact of a canon. He scooped her up and their lips locked as he traversed the few steps through living room to her bedroom. When they reached the door, she dropped a hand to turn the knob and open it. She slid down along his body, and together they tossed all the packages that had covered the bed to the floor.

She laughed, a throaty, sultry laugh, contagious, and inviting.

He held her again.

"Jack," she whispered against his ear, then gently bit his earlobe. Her fingers worked the buttons on his shirt, pulling it out of his pants. She reached for his belt.

A train surged through his head, blood pounding, heart racing. He wanted her more than he'd ever wanted a woman. His hands slipped under her blouse and along her silken skin. The curve of her hips, the sound of her breath, her body pressed against his, urgent and inviting. He thought he would explode.

Together they sank to the bed, then she lay back and he lay atop her. Their kisses grew long and deep; they couldn't get enough of each other.

"I've wanted you since I first saw you," he whispered.

She moaned and he found heaven.

LAYLA HAD NEVER WANTED a man more. Not Mark Ross, who had left her at the altar, and certainly not Seth Thomas. No one had moved her like Jack. *Jack. Jack. Jack.* Even his name moved her. She had never intended for this to happen. He was supposed to drop her off and leave her alone. Forever. But she couldn't fight the desire any longer. She'd thought she'd burst with it.

His mouth moved along her throat, her collarbone, to the rise of her breast. How much more could she take? She moved with his rhythm, unable to stop herself. She looked down at the top of his head, and he gazed up at her, smiling, his blue eyes now dark with passion, the color of the wine-dark sea. He moved back up and captured her mouth.

How could she let this happen? How could she not? She'd vowed never to let anyone in again, but she couldn't resist him. It was as if something within her had been calling for years, and he was the answer to her call. But what about the hurt? Loving someone always ended in hurt. Maybe not this time. Maybe this time loving will be good and kind and gentle.

Their bodies strained together, and she let go of all her doubts and fears. She let herself go with reckless abandon, ignoring the tiny voice that kept repeating, "But what if you get hurt again?" She didn't care. All she cared about was being in his arms, feeling beautiful, feeling safe.

A deep, guttural moan came from his throat, thrilling her, bringing her to the edge. She floated, overcome with ecstasy and release, hearing his passion answer hers. They moved together until they were spent, then collapsed into a blissful embrace.

She lay curled against him, her head on his shoulder, cradled in his arm. With his other hand he softly caressed her cheek, then kissed the top of her head.

"You're amazing," he whispered.

"So are you."

They lay in silence for a few minutes.

"Our soup is probably cold."

She lifted her head to look at him. "Are you thinking of food right now?"

He laughed and traced the curve of her hip. "Not at all." He kissed her.

She lay back against his shoulder. In a few minutes he snored softly, and she smiled.

Maybe this time.

TWENTY-FOUR

Layla drifted awake when Jack stirred.

So, this wasn't a dream.

When she opened her eyes, he was watching her with such care that her heart clutched. She ran her finger along his jaw, and he lifted her fingers and pressed them to his lips, holding them there.

The early morning sun slanted through the blinds, wrapping them in the golden hour glow. A soft spring breeze floated through the slightly opened window and mixed with the scent of jasmine from the unlit candle on the nightstand. Layla lost herself in the warmth and scent of the room and the afterglow of their lovemaking.

"You're beautiful."

She had never believed that, even when Mark had told her. Of course, Dad had told her, but he was Dad and he was supposed to say that. But when Jack said it, she believed it. Inside and out, she felt beautiful—was beautiful.

She kissed him, slow and long.

He caressed her body, kissed her neck, her shoulders.

"Is this how you play doctor?" she teased.

His body stiffened, and he pulled back. He sat up.

"Layla, I don't know how you got the idea I'm a doctor, but I'm not."

Her brow creased. She pictured him entering her hospital room, fixing her IV, checking her stats. The picture didn't match his words.

"What?"

"I'm not a doctor. I never said I was a doctor. And every time you said that, and I tried to explain, someone or something interrupted." He sat up. "Every damn time."

His face had changed from languid to intense. "I never meant to mislead you. I still don't know why you thought I was a doctor."

"But ... but ... you came into my hospital room and took care of me." She was off balance, shifting so quickly from the serenity of being in his arms to these confusing words. "Why did you even come into my room if you weren't my doctor? Are you a nurse?"

"I came in to see how you were doing. I was concerned about you." He took her hand and kissed it.

"Why? You didn't even know me."

Now his brows knit in confusion. "Yes, I did."

"When did we meet?" She cast her mind back to meetings she'd had with other lawyers since joining the firm. Try as she might, she couldn't place him—and she was sure she'd remember his face.

"I came into your office that day."

A slow dread slipped into her gut. She didn't want to hear this; she didn't want to ask.

"That day? What day?" She pulled her hand away.

"The day you got the first threat. The day you opened the envelope with the powder."

She skittered away from him, clutching the sheet to her breast. "No. No. No."

Though he reached out, she moved back farther.

The memory of her face reflected in his mask hit her with full force. The dread, the fear and vulnerability. He had seen her as she never wanted anyone to see her.

"Get out," she growled. "Get out now!" she shrieked.

Jack jumped up, hands outstretched, beseeching. "I tried to tell you. I didn't lie to you. What's wrong, Layla?"

She stood, trembling, a vein throbbing in her temple. "Get out, Jack."

Jack threw his clothes on, hopping on one foot at a time to put on his shoes. All the while saying, "It's all right, Layla. We can work this out. Please, let's talk about it."

She stepped back, arms clasping the wrapped sheet, glaring at him.

As he straightened to leave, he tried one more time. "Layla ...."

But she interrupted him, croaking out, "I never want to see you again."

He stood, hands outstretched in supplication. He dropped them and stalked out of her bedroom. The condo door closed, and his steps retreated down the stairs.

Maybe not this time either.

TWENTY-FIVE

Layla moved like a robot. Bend, pick up a package, lay it on the rumpled bed. Bend, pick, up a package, lay it on the rumpled bed. If she moved like a robot, maybe she wouldn't feel anguish either. Maybe the sharp pain in her heart would disappear and she'd be able to take a deep breath again. Maybe the little men with hammers would stop pounding them in her head. She tightened the belt of her robe.

No more packages to pick up. Hang up the dress. Set aside the lingerie. On she went with one rote movement after another. All she really wanted to do was curl up in her bed. But returning to the bed meant lying on warm sheets where Jack had been just minutes before. Where his scent of sandalwood would linger on the pillowcase, the wrinkled fabric testament to his presence.

Put away the accessories. One piece at a time.

Coffee. She needed coffee and to get ready for work. Ugh. The thought of facing the gauntlet sharpened the pain in her head.

The kitchen still held the aroma of Miss Ida's delicious—though untouched—soup and bread. The bowls sat accusingly, spoons still balanced on the rims, the table askew from their impassioned embrace and rush to the bedroom.

She rubbed her eyes, stretching them in a way would bring on early wrinkles. What did she care? *Bring on wrinkles, bring on gray hair, bring whatever you have in store for me. I'm through.*

Miss Ida's door opened and closed, and she waited for the knock. There it was.

Maybe if I'm quiet, she'll go away.

"Layla? Are you all right?" She knocked again.

Layla held her breath.

"I'll just stand here and knock until you open this door, girl."

It was no use. She'd never been able to out-wait Miss Ida. She unlocked the door and stood aside.

Miss Ida entered and glanced toward the bedroom. "'Bout damn time," she muttered.

Layla closed her eyes.

With her hands on her hips, Miss Ida inspected the kitchen table. "Mmm, mmm, mmm. I know my soup wasn't that bad, so, girl, he must be hot."

"Miss Ida, please ...."

The woman finally took a long look at Layla. "Uh-oh. It didn't end well. I wondered when I heard your door slam."

She shook her head. "No, it sure didn't."

Miss Ida patted her arm, then led her to the sofa. "I can listen all day if you need." She wrapped an arm around Layla's shoulders and drew her in. She pulled out a fresh hankie and handed it to her. Miss Ida always had a fresh hankie in her pocket.

Layla waved it away. She sat up and Miss Ida held her hand.

"You don't have to tell me anything. Whatever you need. If you just need me to sit here with you awhile, I can do that."

Layla was back in eighth grade when Stephen Farrell broke up with her in the middle of the dance floor during the Spring Fling. All of her friends had witnessed her humiliation. Wrapped in her mother's arms, she'd bawled out what she was sure was the greatest tragedy in the world. But Mom's arms had been frail. The cancer was already sucking the life from her, and the despair Layla had been feeling that night was nothing compared to what she would face in the coming months as Mom lay dying.

Miss Ida's arms were strong, bearing her up, giving her support. The loss ripping Layla apart at that moment brought the same end-of-the-world-despair sensation, and she rested in Miss Ida's comfort.

Finally, in a voice reminiscent of her eighth-grade self, she murmured, "I thought I was safe with him."

Miss Ida stroked her hair. "Mmm-hmm."

"I thought he was honest, that I could trust him." She sat up and looked at Miss Ida, whose view was of the bedroom.

"I see that, child."

"He lied to me. He said he was a doctor." Her breath hitched. "But he was the guy in the hazmat suit."

"Ohhh." Miss Ida's eyes widened, and she pursed her lips. "Ohhh."

Just saying the words brought a pit to Layla's stomach, and it lay there, heavy and onerous, a lump of lead. She rubbed her midsection to soothe it away. She tried to conjure up her anger again; in a battle of devastating emotions, anger could oust despair and the black hollow carved within her. But she didn't have the strength to conjure anything right now. She curled up with her head on Miss Ida's shoulder and welcomed the arm that enwrapped her.

"A lie is a hard thing to forgive. That's sure." Miss Ida murmured.

Once again, she pictured Jack entering her hospital room. Though she'd been concentrating on yanking out the IV, she could never forget the first time she saw his piercing blue eyes and irresistible dimples. And with his shirtsleeves rolled part way up his forearms, the shirt the same deep blue as his eyes, his image was seared into her brain. Where was his lab coat? Where was his stethoscope? He hadn't had either.

"Damn." She sat up.

"What is it?"

"He never lied to me about being a doctor. I'd just assumed that he was." She described their first meeting. "So many medical staff had been in and out all day, I assumed he was just one more."

"Well, that's something to consider, isn't it?" Miss Ida patted her hand.

Layla straightened. "But he's still the person in the hazmat suit. He saw me—" How could she describe how naked she'd felt? How vulnerable and humiliated. How she never wanted to face the person who saw her like that.

"Why was he there? In your office?"

Layla looked at her as if she'd asked why the sky was blue.

"Because he...because I..."

On some level, Layla knew the answer and its implication, but she was not ready to let down her barbed wire fence of protection yet. She clung to the belief that he was the bad guy who'd barged in on her in some way. For him, for anyone, to see her that afraid, that vulnerable, made her feel violated. When she let people in, when she cared about them, they left her. She couldn't bear that heartbreak anymore.

After a moment, Miss Ida stood. "If you need me, you know where to find me."

Layla took her hand. "Thanks for being here for me." Her throat tightened, and she swallowed hard.

She lay back on the sofa and Miss Ida covered her with the afghan Mom had made years before. Miss Ida stopped in the kitchen, gathered the dishes from the unfinished dinner, and left, closing the door softly.

Layla's arms lay limp alongside her body. Her legs stretched out, feet poking out at the end of the afghan. Getting up was too much effort, and she could not bear the sight of the rumpled bed. She just needed an hour before she went to work.

As she drifted off to sleep, she thought again, "Not this time. Not ever."

TWENTY-SIX

Jack slapped his last card down on the table. "Shit."

"Man, you're playing like a frickin' kindergartener, Trenton. What bug crawled up your ass?" Steve Warczynski scooped up the last trick gleefully.

"I wish you'd find out so we could start playing euchre, *partner*." PJ O'Keefe glared at Jack.

"No, no. Jack's doing just fine." Nick, Steve's euchre partner, took a long swig of his soda.

"Does it have anything to do with a certain tall, dark-haired woman?" Steve grinned at him.

Jack put both elbows on the table and dropped his head in his hands. "Jesus."

"Oh my God—it does! She got to you. I knew she would!" Steve slapped him on the arm and dealt out the cards. "Spill the details, man."

Jack pulled his head up and scowled at him. The hammer that had been pounding in his head since he'd left Layla's apartment went into overdrive. Now a chainsaw had been added, splitting his skull as he tried to figure out what the hell he'd done to make her so furious. Their time together had been hot—the hottest he'd ever had. He'd been hungry for her, like he couldn't get enough, and the way she kissed him, caressed him—man he had to stop thinking about it or the guys would see just how excited she'd gotten him.

But it wasn't just sex. Being with her was, what? Magic? He'd wanted to please her, to see her passion, to share her smile. For the first time in his life, it wasn't about him—it was about them. It was like they were the only two people in the world. That intimacy was different than any time before. *Geez, I sound like a frickin' romance novel.*

The talking, the dealing, the card playing had stopped and all three guys were looking at him, PJ with disdain, Nick with confusion, and Steve with ... compassion?

Steve murmured, "She more than got to you, didn't she?"

Jack puffed out his cheek and let the breath seep out like a leaky balloon.

"Man." Steve shook his head solemnly.

"She's a broad. There's a million of 'em out there." PJ studied his hand.

"Show some respect, PJ. You're not hanging with your drug buddies right now." Steve picked up his cards and arranged them.

"Oh, yeah. Sorry, Sir Knight." PJ frowned at his cards. Under his breath he said, "Fuck, not only don't I have a decent partner today, I can't get a decent hand."

Jack looked at his cards but may as well have looked at a Greek scroll for all the sense they made. He laid them face down on the table.

"So, we had a really great night, you know? Then, this morning, she starts screaming at me to get out."

"Sounds like she's psycho," PJ fingered the jack of spades that rested on top of the bid pile.

"No, I think she's just been hurt a lot."

Like a beehive, all three listeners made a buzzing noise of acknowledgement in their throats. Steve's sounded like commiseration. Nick's sounded like doubt. PJ's sounded like "let's get on with the card game."

"So, what's your bid?" PJ looked at Nick to his left.

"Pass."

PJ's eyes burned into Jack's. Jack looked at his hand full of red cards. "Pass."

"Fuck." PJ slammed back in his chair.

"Pick it up, shorty," Steve let out a diabolical laugh.

PJ scowled at him, then turned to Jack. "So, what were you two talking about right before she blew up at you?"

Jack figured PJ was trying to delay their inevitable loss, but he'd take any opportunity to get this off his chest.

"We were talking about the day she got the first threat. The letter with powder in it."

Though Steve and PJ knew about the incident, Nick didn't. He stared at Jack as if he were speaking a foreign language.

"She's been threatened. Actually, she's being stalked. Listen, she doesn't want to talk about it, so it's not my story to tell."

PJ sat forward. "Wait a minute. Is she that lawyer broad? Where you were the first responder for hazmat?"

Jack bit his lip, then nodded.

PJ looked around like he'd discovered gold. "Hey, I met her!" He bestowed an appreciative look at Jack. "She's hot. Nice going."

Jack rubbed his eyes. "Jesus. It wasn't like that. She's ...." How could he describe her, what they'd had together? Her heart jumped. *Maybe it's just a heart attack.*

Steve led the jack of clubs, forcing PJ to play his higher jack of spades. Steve snickered as PJ let another f-bomb fly. PJ slapped down the king of hearts, Nick played the nine, Jack played the ace, and Steve trumped it with the ten of spades. "You're going down." He laid down the rest of his hand—all spades—and the stream of obscenities that exploded from PJ flooded the room.

Usually, Jack would join in cursing with PJ, but he didn't have it in him. His hands rested on the table because if they didn't, they'd simply hang by his side. All the strength, all the energy, all the passion he'd felt that morning had deflated like a leaky balloon. He may as well be a puddle on the floor.

"So why was she mad that you were there to save her life?" Steve tucked the deck of cards into its box.

Jack rubbed the back of his neck, recalling the conversation for the hundredth time since he'd left. "That made her madder than when I finally explained to her that I wasn't a doctor."

PJ sat forward, clasping his hands on the table as if he were a professor about to explain a theory to his students. "Wait a minute. You told this chick that you were a doctor?" He leaned back in his chair. "Great line, man."

"No!" Jack thought steam must be coming out his ears. "How many times will I have to explain this? I am not a doctor." Firefighters watching TV in the next room turned to look at him.

"We know that, Jack," one yelled over the drug commercial.

"Geez." Jack threw his head back and stared at the ceiling.

"Okay, so you told her you weren't a doctor ... for whatever reason ... and then you told her you maybe saved her life. And that's when she got mad at you?" Steve scratched his head.

Jack rolled his eyes at him.

Steve held out his hands. "Seriously, man. I'm just trying to help here."

Jack took a deep breath and let it out slowly. "Yes. That's when she got angry and told me to get out. Shouted it, actually."

PJ's eyes twinkled, and he opened his mouth, but Steve shot him a warning glance, and he kept quiet, though his leg jiggled under the table.

"It doesn't make sense." Steve scratched his chin.

"Okay, she's a chick. Don't expect her to make sense." PJ leaned his chair back, balancing it on the rear legs.

All three men glared at him.

"What?" PJ's eyes were round with innocence.

"I just need to think—" Jack rubbed his eyes.

The alarm sounded, and PJ slammed his chair down. The other three men were up and moving in an instant.

I need to let this go. I need to concentrate now. But the image of Layla, of the hurt in her eyes, haunted him as he ran to his truck.

TWENTY-SEVEN

Friday, May 22

Layla stared at her reflection. At Miss Ida's insistence, she'd gone to a salon for the whole package: hair styled, manicure, pedicure, makeup. She felt like a poodle who'd just gotten clipped and had to face all the dogs in the park.

But this was for Isaiah and Miss Ida. Tonight was Isaiah's big celebration.

With her hair swept up and just a few strands softening around her temples, her face looked delicate. Her eyes popped with the expert application of shadow, mascara, and the pièce de résistance: eyeliner, which the stylist had stroked up at the corners to give her eyes a seductive tilt.

When she put on the coral dress, she thought of Cinderella. And Monique was her fairy godmother. The silken fabric, the perfect fit. But when she looked in the mirror, she gasped. She hadn't realized how the new bra she'd purchased would lift her breasts so much that they rounded above the bodice of her dress. The modest décolletage in the dressing room mirror had transformed to seductress in her bedroom mirror. She ran to her closet to retrieve the black dress but stopped. The fairy godmother had kept it—clever woman. She'd anticipated just such an occurrence.

A knock came on her door.

"I'm waiting for you, darlin','" Miss Ida called. "We've got to go or I'll miss my son's award ceremony." She knocked again.

Layla glanced in the mirror again. She smiled at herself. *You look stunning, Layla.*

"Come on, child. We got to go *now.*"

At the last minute, she grabbed her new black wrap with silver threads shot through it and draped it around her shoulders.

At least she wouldn't know anyone there.

JACK LEANED AGAINST THE BAR, tugging at his bowtie. Who invented clothing like this? A torture expert? He yanked at the cummerbund of his tuxedo. Give him his usual khakis and polo shirts or open collar dress shirts and he was a happy man. He looked in the mirror above the bar. He had to admit he cleaned up well. *I showered and brushed my teeth. Not bad. I wouldn't scare women away. Except one.* He downed his scotch.

Steve was beside him.

Jack nodded at him. "Where have you been?" Jack signaled the bartender for another.

"Anywhere you aren't. Geez, standing next to you is the worst place to be. It's like putting a Chevy Corvair next to a Porsche."

Jack tucked a couple of bills in the tip jar and nodded his thanks to the bartender. He squinted at Steve. "Are you calling me a Corvair?'"

Steve stared at him. "You don't even know, do you?"

"Know what?"

"Know how you look with your frickin' blue eyes and perfect black hair. Geez, you're 007 in that goddamn tux."

A woman with coppery hair and alabaster skin approached. She tucked her arm through Steve's, but her eyes never left Jack.

"Hi, Steve."

"Hi, Amber."

She stood silent, looking at Jack. He smiled at her as he took in her beauty. But she was too short, and her skin looked pasty, not the rosy hue Layla's took on when she looked up from lying beneath him, a smile playing on her face. And the red hair meant a temper, right? Not the deep brown that signaled a milder temper. Oh wait. Wasn't Layla just screaming at him to get out a couple of days ago?

Stop. Stop comparing women to her. There will never be another...

That thought buckled his knees, and he grabbed the bar to keep from collapsing.

This made the woman giggle.

Ugh. She giggles, too. Stop!

Steve finally relented and introduced them. After some small talk that made it apparent Jack wasn't going to pursue her, the woman meandered off.

"See? That's what I mean."

Jack squinted at him. "I don't get you, man."

"I've known her for three years. I've asked her out, but she's never accepted. Then you show up, she doesn't know you from Adam, and she's ready to sleep with you now. Oh, and you gave her just enough encouragement to keep her on the hook for a while."

"What? I didn't encourage her!"

"Oh, what was that little dip you did when she was standing her? As if she was so beautiful you were falling for her."

Jack leaned into his face, spitting out his words. "That wasn't about her."

Steve eyed Jack's half-full Scotch glass.

"No, I'm not drunk. And, no, you're not a Corvair." Jack drained his drink and slammed the glass down. People near them jumped and threw disapproving looks. Jack waved. "Sorry." They returned to their conversations. He turned and rested against the bar and muttered, "If you must know, I was comparing her to Layla, and it shook me up."

Steve jerked his head back like a curious chicken. "That's serious." He aped Jack's stance and the two stared into the mirror behind the bar. "There are a lot of beautiful women here tonight."

"You can have them all. All but—" He jerked up, almost toppling the barstool beside him, still focused on the mirror. "Layla."

"Yeah. I knew who you meant." Steve signaled for drinks for both of them.

"No. I mean Layla." His voice was reverent.

"Geez, I know. You don't have to explain. I may be a Corvair, but I'm an intelligent Corvair."

"Shh," Jack hissed as if Steve's words could be heard above the din of people. "She's here."

Steve looked in the mirror. "Dude, that's Isaiah's mother. But, holy shit, who is with her?"

They looked at each other and spoke as one. "Layla."

Steve looked back in the mirror. "Even a Porsche isn't good enough for her."

Jack didn't hear him. His eyes were glued to the mirror, his mind full of her gentle laugh while they made love, of her eyes, soft with passion, her kiss that set him on fire.

His breath caught as he gaped at her image in the mirror. She had stopped beneath a light, golden highlights shimmering along the sweep of her chestnut hair. The dress she wore hugged all the curves he remembered caressing, and her skin glowed against the color—what was it? Not pink, not orange. Salmon? Her legs went on forever until high, spiky heels arched her foot in a way that made him plunk down on his barstool.

But though she smiled through introductions, her face revealed sadness. He could tell. Jack had seen her light up with love for Clarence, with ecstasy in his own arms, but no joy was evident tonight. Anyone who didn't know her would simply see fine cheekbones and deep-set brown eyes, and if the person were close enough, they'd see gold flecks in them that matched the highlights in her hair. Her eyes burned in his memory.

Steve punched his arm. "Take a breath."

Jack threw him a look of "don't bother me now" but realized he hadn't taken a breath since Layla had entered. He inhaled and returned his gaze to the mirror.

"I can see why you're smitten, Porsche. She's drop-dead sexy."

Jack snorted. "I've never seen her all done up like this." *I never needed to.* "She's even more beautiful." He cleared his throat.

Steve patted his shoulder. "I hope you can work it out, Jack."

Jack downed his drink. "Thanks, Steve. So do I."

He looked back at the mirror. *You don't know how much.*

LAYLA FELT like a cardboard paper doll, the kind she used to play with as a girl. She could dress it up in all kinds of fancy outfits, but it was still a paper doll. Cardboard. Her mouth was beginning to tire from the smile she'd pasted on, but she would gut her way through this for Miss Ida. Faces and names floated by her as she was introduced to police officers, firefighters, and other first responders. All here to celebrate Isaiah.

She smiled genuinely now as she remembered that. Isaiah and Miss Ida, that's what this night was all about. No matter her discomfort in this crowd, no matter how many faces and names she was supposed to remember, she would be as charming and friendly as she could be to make this night special for them. *Even if it kills me.* She smiled and shook another hand.

Isaiah whistled when he caught site of her.

"Why, thank you, son." Miss Ida offered her cheek.

He laughed and kissed her. "You look drop-dead gorgeous, Mama."

She pulled back and gave him a look. "Goodness, I hope not. I'm not ready to meet my Maker yet." She kissed him back.

He grinned at Layla, eyes dancing. "You don't look half bad either, Ms. Forrester."

Layla warmed. "Thank you, Isaiah." She hugged him, noting over his broad shoulder, that several men nearby stared at her in admiration. When she stepped back, she reached for the black silk wrap she'd carried, but Miss Ida whisked it away and stuffed it in her own huge handbag. Then she gave Layla the stink eye.

Isaiah took his mother's arm. "Let's get you ladies a beverage." He led them toward the bar.

Layla stopped dead in her tracks, causing another guest to bump into her.

Jack.

She stared at the back of his head. She'd know the ebony sheen and wave of his hair from any angle. She'd seen it from many. He couldn't have seen her; he hadn't turned around. Then her gaze travelled to the mirror and met his. A knife through the heart couldn't have pierced her any harder. She sucked in her breath.

Even James Bond wasn't that handsome in his tuxedo. Jack's blue eyes pierced hers in his reflection. Clean shaven, hair more under control than usual, his bow tie straight, he could have posed for GQ. Her legs turned to Jell-O, and she stumbled.

Isaiah caught her by the elbow. "Hey, you haven't even had your first drink yet." He followed her gaze. "You know Jack?"

She nodded.

"Cool. Let's go say hello."

"No!" She broke away from Jack's gaze and looked at Isaiah. "I need the ladies' room. Would you please order me a cabernet? No. Make it a martini." She couldn't help it. Her eyes strayed back to the mirror. Jack's gaze hadn't left her. *Oh God.* The conversations in the hall rose and fell in a mesmerizing cacophony. The room swam and a trickle of sweat meandered along her spine. She had to get out of here now.

Miss Ida took Layla's arm. "Get me a martini, too."

"But, Mama, you don't drink."

"Then get me a ginger ale as well." She called as she steered Layla toward the ladies' room.

They entered the lounge that led to the restroom, and Miss Ida eased her onto one of the ridiculously small, round, tufted velvet chairs. She sat on the next one. Taking Layla's hands in her own, she leaned forward.

"I saw him. And I know your heart is breaking. If you want to leave, Isaiah can bring me home. But, Layla, it would mean so much to me if you would stay. Isaiah getting this award, well, it's a bigger deal to me than you can imagine." She patted her hands. "I'm going back now. If I don't see you, I'll understand. If I do, you've got two martinis waiting for you." She winked and left.

Layla's stomach lurched, and she ran into a stall in the restroom. She didn't vomit, but she wished she would. Maybe this churning would stop. *Come on, he's just a guy. You're giving him too much control.*

She paused at the sink to wash her hands and pat her neck with a cool paper towel. She drilled into her reflection. *You've got this. You can get through this night. For Isaiah. For Miss Ida. Be cool. He's just a guy.* A soft voice, from somewhere deeper within, whispered, *Yes, a guy you're in love with.*

She threw the towel down. "No, I'm not!"

A startled woman paused in her exit from the stall behind her.

Layla attempted a smile. "Sorry."

The woman edged toward a sink farther down, her eyes peering sideways at Layla while she washed her hands.

Layla returned to the jovial atmosphere of the celebration, the noise and jollity having increased with the duration of the cocktail hour. She searched for Miss Ida and spotted her holding a ginger ale in one hand and a delicate martini glass in the other.

"'Bout time you got here." Miss Ida tried to sound tough, but the smile in her eyes gave her away. She handed Layla the martini. "Thank you, child," she whispered.

Layla hugged her, then steeled herself for what was inevitable. Jack.

Isaiah held a beer and another martini. "Let's find our table." He led them through the maze of half-filled round tables until a short man who yanked at his collar and looked like he'd rather be anywhere but in his tuxedo met them.

"Isaiah, you're at the front, man. What did you expect?"

Layla's jaw dropped. This was the homeless man who'd been at the police station when she'd filed a report with Isaiah. Her head spun. This night was getting stranger and stranger.

"Hey, thanks, PJ."

"No problem. I'm back here with the unwashed masses." PJ pointed to a table nearby.

"You're always with the unwashed masses, dude." Isaiah laughed.

"I prefer it to this ... this ... suit." PJ stretched the collar out again and tugged the pants in the rear.

Actually, he was quite attractive all cleaned up. His long, red hair was pulled back in a ponytail, and he actually smelled minty. He hadn't shaved his five o'clock shadow, but that lent him a rugged Hollywood action-film aura. If Isaiah hadn't been towering almost a foot above him, he wouldn't have appeared so short. But his stocky figure and pugnacious attitude atoned for his lack of height.

Isaiah introduced PJ to his mother who insisted he simply call her Miss Ida. He smiled at her like an eighth-grade boy trying to impress his teacher. Layla expected him to pull an apple out of his tux pocket, polish it on his cummerbund, and present it to her.

Miss Ida grinned back. "I've heard about your adventures, PJ. Some mighty fine crime fighting going on with you."

Layla was back on the Tilt-a-whirl. *PJ is in law enforcement?* She frowned trying to make sense of it all.

He finally looked at her. "Still don't approve, Miss Forrester? I took a bath and combed my hair."

Isaiah's laugh was a low rumble that built until he threw his head back.

"Hello, PJ. You look very nice this evening." Why did she sound like a robot whenever she spoke to him?

Because he looks like what my stalker should look like, and that makes me want to slug him.

Because he doesn't give a rat's ass what people think of him, and that annoys me.

She attempted a genuine smile, but then Jack and another man approached and stood behind him. Her smile faded.

"Well, your approval didn't last long." PJ grinned and winked at Isaiah.

She looked back at him. "No, no, it isn't about you—"

"Are we breaking up already?" PJ tilted his head.

"Hello, Layla." Jack appeared behind PJ.

"Ahh ..." PJ nodded and stepped aside.

Jack stepped forward.

His voice sounded in her ears but echoed in her heart. All the people faded away. All the noise became an ocean-depth din. Her skin tingled as it had when he'd caressed her. She pushed down every tiny sensation his words, his gaze, his presence elicited and tightened every muscle in her body.

"Hello, Jack." Robot voice.

The rest of the group melted away, so they stood alone.

"Layla, I'm sor—"

"Stop." She held up her hand. "This is Isaiah's night. And Miss Ida's."

He nodded.

"Yes. But we need to talk. I need to understand—"

A woman on the stage went to the dais and took the microphone, causing it to screech until she moved it away from the speaker. Behind her, instruments were set for a four-piece band.

Oh, no. Not dancing. Layla pressed her stomach to stem the heebie-jeebies.

The woman shouted into the mic, "Good evening. We'll start serving dinner and begin tonight's presentation in about ten minutes, so please find your table and have a seat."

Layla was grateful for the interruption. It gave her time to regain her composure.

Again, the woman boomed through the speaker. "If everyone would please take their seats now."

The room came alive again for Layla, and she and Jack were the only two standing. Mortified, she looked left, then right. She had no idea where she was supposed to sit. Jack reached for her elbow to escort her to her seat.

"I don't know where I'm supposed to be." Sweat broke out on her forehead. Then she spotted Isaiah approaching.

He took her arm and escorted her to the empty chair next to Miss Ida at the front table. Her face flushed as she imagined everyone's eyes on her. *One more reason to stay away from you, Jack Trenton.*

TWENTY-EIGHT

Miss Ida smiled broadly, and her eyes sparkled with pride as Isaiah's accomplishments were read. Her hand fluttered to her chest when the Chief of Police presented him the Grand Rapids Police Department Medal of Valor.

The chief described Isaiah's heroic rescue of a child who had fallen through the ice on the Grand River in February. He happened to be onsite and reached her before the rescue squad arrived. He'd saved the child's life, but as a result, he'd been hospitalized for injuries and severe hypothermia.

Isaiah's speech was both eloquent and humble as he credited his fellow law enforcement colleagues for their support of his efforts, noting any of them would have done the same.

Finally, he looked at Miss Ida.

"Of all the people I owe this award to, the most important is my mother, Ida Jefferson. Mom, your belief in me, your sacrifices to make sure I got the education I needed to pursue my dreams, and most of all, your insistence on truth and integrity are why I stand here today. This award is as much yours as mine, and I thank you." He held up the award and blew a kiss to her.

The room erupted with a burst of applause and the sound of chairs scraping the floor as the audience stood, clapping. Loud shouts of "Bravo" and a chant of "Is-a-iah" sounded and above it all, a shrill whistle and then, "You're the baddest ass of all, man!"

Layla recognized PJ and paraphrased a line from Shakespeare: *He be but small, but he be fierce.* She pursed her lips to the side, trying to tamp down her increasing affection for him.

While waitstaff cleared dessert plates and coffee cups, the band assembled. A blonde singer in a sequined dress launched into a sultry rendition of "The Look of Love."

The pit that had resisted every morsel Layla forced into her stomach now grew to baseball size, and she checked the path and distance to the ladies' room, just in case. Of course, she was at the table farthest from the restroom. That's how this evening was going.

The crowd was warming to the band, and a duet of "Uptown Funk" got people dancing. Then the male singer sang "Don't Stop Believin'," and Isaiah bowed to Miss Ida, who eagerly took his hand and headed out to the dance floor.

This song was one of Layla's favorites, but tonight, she wasn't sure what she believed in anymore. Deserted at the table, she decided to visit—no, hide in—the ladies' room, but someone thwarted her plan.

"You look stunning this evening, Layla." Roland Gage sat beside her, but not before she caught him focused on her décolletage. Taking her hand, he kissed it, lingering too long, his hot, moist breath turning her stomach. She withdrew her hand from his, resisting the urge to wipe it on her napkin.

"How are you? I was out of town when you experienced that shocking incident at the office."

But a letter containing powder could have been prepared before you left. She held his gaze, watching him struggle to not look at her breasts. She might have laughed if she weren't trapped by him, his leg pushed up against hers beneath the table.

"We have much to discuss about your opportunities at the firm. Why don't we meet somewhere, say drinks after work on Monday?" His eyes glittered and she thought of the Big Bad Wolf in cartoons.

"I think any business discussion should take place during business hours, Roland."

The trace of a frown flicked in his face, but he recovered. "A more relaxed atmosphere might open up possibilities we hadn't thought of at the office." His offer slid to her, oily and repulsive. She reached for her napkin, catching site of an elegant woman in a sequined jacket glaring at them. Her nostrils flared and she tapped her fingers on the table.

"Is that lovely woman your wife, Roland? I believe she wants to dance with you."

He turned to look, withdrawing his leg from beside hers. His voice was low. "You'd best think about what you want in life, Layla." He spoke louder. "Fine, Ms. Forrester, but let's discuss work during business hours." He rose and headed toward the furious woman.

I believe I would not be your first dalliance, Mr. Gage. But what are the consequences if I say no? More threats? More danger? Have you already laid the groundwork?

"May I have this dance?"

PJ O'Keefe startled her. She considered his offer. Did she want to tower over him as he led her through whatever dance steps he might know in front of all these people? In front of Jack? But his smile was dazzling.

"Sure."

He pulled out her chair and led her to the floor next to Isaiah and Miss Ida, who winked her approval.

Layla loved to dance but seldom had the opportunity since

dating was on her list of strictly forbidden things. Another problem with her fling with Seth had been that he didn't dance. Her one opportunity and it didn't work out. Story of that brief romance.

PJ, on the other hand, obviously was in his element, and he had the moves to prove it. The song faded into "Soul Man," and PJ took her hand and led her through the swing. He held her waist and grasped her hand firmly enough to guide her through the steps.

Shouts of "PJ, you badass," and "Whoa, check out PJ Astaire," mixed with catcalls and hoots. PJ just smiled broader and danced smoother. Layla smiled, too, a smile that might crack her face it was so unaccustomed to such a stretch. A laugh bubbled up and spilled out. She didn't look at the guys teasing PJ, which normally would have sent her flying to her car and straight home. PJ had a strange effect on her. His disregard for what others thought, his determination to grab life by the scruff of the neck and shake delight from it, was contagious.

She quickly learned the pattern of the dance, and followed him with ease, twirling beneath his arm, cupping alongside him in matched steps, hand on his shoulder, dipping and swaying. She soared with the music and the movement, alive, expansive, like an eagle circling the sea. Did she have wings?

When the song stopped, she held her hand to her chest to slow her breathing, trying to not let her disappointment show on her face. PJ bowed courteously and held out his arm to escort her back to the table.

"May I cut in?" A tall, lanky man with tawny hair and green eyes bowed slightly. She'd noticed him sitting next to Jack at the bar when she'd entered. Her eyes flicked in search of Jack and located him dancing with a svelte redhead, his back to her. Stung by a pang of jealousy, she raised her chin to meet his green eyes. "Yes. Thank you."

As PJ lowered his arm, he made introductions. "Miss Forrester, may I present Steven Warczynski?"

Steve shot PJ a look like he'd just exited an alien spacecraft. "What the hell is with you?"

PJ frowned. "Watch your language in front of a lady." Then he swaggered away stretched to his full five foot five, head high, shoulders thrown back as the next song, a slow dance, filled the room.

Steve took her hand and led her back to the floor. Slipping his arm around her waist, he held her at a respectful distance. Unlike with PJ, Layla had to look up at Steve—would he be able to hear her if she spoke? Also, unlike PJ, Steve basically danced in one place in a circle.

"How do you know Isaiah?" His bass voice was easy to hear.

She glanced to where Isaiah was dancing with a woman cop she'd seen at the station and who had exchanged her uniform for a gorgeous gold lamé dress. There was no respectful distance between them. She looked up at Steve. "Miss Ida is my neighbor. I've gotten to know Isaiah through her. He's like my brother."

Steve smiled. "Cool."

As they pivoted in place, she spotted PJ dancing with Miss Ida. He held her regally and danced as smoothly as Fred Astaire. Miss Ida's face was alight with pleasure, her smile radiant.

I'm so glad I stayed. It's worth it just to see her face right now.

Layla didn't feel disappointed at the end of this dance. A bit dizzy perhaps. But though their conversation had been light, underneath she stayed on alert knowing he was Jack's friend. Another slow song drifted to her, and someone tapped on her shoulder.

"May I have this dance?"

A tickle of heat slithered along her back and spread warmth through her body. She turned to be captured by ocean-blue eyes that beckoned her to say yes. A war raged within her—her mind screaming no! Her body begging yes! Without having to look, she knew several sets of eyes were on her and Jack at that moment. Had all of this been a set up? She glanced at the exit. Isaiah could bring Miss Ida home.

"Yes." She moved into his arms.

His arm burned her waist where it rested against the fabric of her dress. Her disloyal hand lay in his as if it had found a home, warm and safe. Like Steve, he held her at a respectful distance, but unlike Steve, his steps were smooth, leading her so her body followed with ease.

"Clapton's right."

"What?" Without thinking, she met his gaze. *Danger. Danger.*

"You look wonderful tonight."

She broke eye contact. "Thank you." Of course she recognized the lyric.

As if reading her mind, he chuckled. "I wondered if that's where your name came from."

She resumed staring at his chin. "Yes. Mom and Dad were rabid fans of Clapton. First live concert I ever went to was his Unplugged tour. Mom practically swooned over that version of 'Layla.' Dad liked the original." *I was probably conceived during that song.* In an effort to quickly erase that image, she glanced at him. "You look good, too. Nice suit. Tuxedo." *Stop sounding like an idiot.*

"Layla, look, I don't know what I said or did to upset you the other day, but whatever I said, I'm sorry. I'd like to make it up to you somehow."

How? By going back in time and not being the guy in the hazmat suit?

"I don't know what you can do."

"At least tell me how I hurt you."

The dance floor swayed with couples in all stages of embrace, all of them vying for room, and Jack and Layla danced in the center, closer and closer as the others crushed them together. Now his cheek rested against hers, and the familiar tug of desire and escape engulfed her.

"I can't tell you. It's ... it's too complicated. But I do now realize you didn't lie to me. I apologize for accusing you of lying. I assumed you were a doctor when you came to my hospital room. I didn't know you were ..." She squeezed her eyes closed against the memory.

Another couple pushed against them, pressing her closer to Jack. The memory of his naked body so close to hers brought the tension between desire and fleeing to an unbearable ache in her chest.

"I'm sorry. Whatever I did to hurt you, I'm sorry." His mouth touched her ear, his whisper soft and warm.

She fought the shiver that ran along every nerve in her body. She wanted to forgive him, to say everything was okay, let's get out of here and be alone. But the image of her terrified face in his mask assaulted all the warmth his words and nearness had ignited in her. She leaned back, pushing against his arm that held her close.

Their eyes met for a moment.

His were mystified.

The song ended. Another ballad began, and no sooner had they parted than the redhead was at Jack's side. She tucked her arm through his, hugging it to her breast. "Me next, Jack."

His eyes never left Layla as the other woman wrapped both arms around his neck.

She dragged her gaze from him and headed toward her table.

Layla, you're a fool.

JACK STOOD with the redhead draped over him as Layla returned to her table. She moved like a river, gracefully flowing, effortless, driven by nature. She whispered to Miss Ida, who nodded her head. Layla caught his gaze, then quickly looked away. She picked up her purse and a black scarf and headed for the door.

Hey, aren't you supposed to leave a glass slipper behind so I can find you again?

What the hell kind of thought was that? He'd lost her forever. And he didn't know why. Hot anger stirred within him, and he let it flow. Anger was easier to take than this hollowness in his gut.

At least you could have told me what the hell I did.

The redhead pressed against him, wrapping her arms tighter. He glanced at her, then pulled her in close.

"Mmmm. Nice, baby." She purred a mixture of desire and triumph.

Her perfume made his stomach lurch. He held her closer. He was going to drink a lot tonight.

THERE'D BEEN TOO many damn cops around last night to get close to her. Even though he'd followed her right into the parking lot, he'd stayed in his car, watching her arrive in her fancy-ass dress. He had to admit she'd looked pretty hot. He let his mind linger on her for a few minutes.

Plus, she was with that old woman. Something told him to stay away. From the number of people arriving, this shindig was going to last all night. So he'd left.

He stared at the photo in the magazine article. There would be other opportunities. And he'd hit her where it hurt the most.

TWENTY-NINE

Saturday, May 23

"Hi, sweetie." Clarence grinned and held out his arms for a hug. "You're up early after the party last night."

"Morning, Dad." Layla embraced him and kissed his cheek. She forced back a yawn. She'd yawned all the way over during the pre-dawn drive. At best she'd gotten two hours of sleep. "I wouldn't miss our fishing date for anything. Dawn is when they're biting."

"How was Isaiah's big bash last night? I saw a clip on the eleven o'clock news. I looked for you, but I didn't see you." He patted the chair beside him. "Tell me about it."

She avoided his penetrating gaze and sat down.

Layla described the presentation and Isaiah's speech. She talked about how Miss Ida glowed as her son was honored. She went into great detail about the delicious dinner, the beautiful place settings, Miss Ida dancing the night away.

He nodded and smiled as she talked, but his gaze pierced her. She tried not to twist her fingers or pull at her ponytail, but she found herself doing both. Repeatedly.

"And how about you, Layla? Did you dance the night away?"

"I danced a few times."

"Oh?"

He wasn't going to let her off the hook. Dad's concern for her love life was a frequent topic of conversation usually ending with, "I don't want you to be a workaholic who ends up with a fat pension and an empty bed."

"Okay. So, I danced with a guy named PJ who I previously thought was homeless, but he was in a tuxedo and danced really well. And I danced with Steve, who went around in circles and made me dizzy." If she talked fast enough maybe she could change the subject and not think about dancing with Jack. "Are you ready to head to Riverside Park? The fish are biting." The thought made her stomach queasy. Pounding down the last of her bottle of moscato when she'd gotten home last night had not been her best idea. She swallowed and took a deep breath to still her stomach.

Dad's quizzical look stopped her litany.

"What are you talking about? You danced with a homeless man in a tuxedo?"

She leaned her head back and breathed deeply. "No ..." she drew the word out, "he isn't homeless. I guess he's some kind of cop. Undercover maybe. They were all cops or firefighters. You know, first responders."

"So, Jack was there?"

Never, ever had she been able to keep things from her father. Even as a kid when she thought she was being so sneaky, he'd find out. Like the night she climbed out her bedroom window to meet some friends, and when she got back well after midnight and climbed in, he was sitting in her desk chair waiting for her. He always saw right through her.

"Yes, Jack was there." She crossed her arms and sat back farther.

"And did you dance with him?"

She rolled her eyes. "Yes, I danced with Jack."

"Good! Did you invite him to join us today? I think he'd enjoy it."

She bolted upright in her seat "No!" Even she was surprised at her reaction, but she wasn't surprised that the pounding in her head returned. She rubbed her temples. Were his eyes twinkling? Seldom did she get angry with Dad, but he was taking this too far.

He held up his hands to ward off her wrath, the sparkle in his eyes fading to concern. "What's up, Sliver? Frankly, you don't look so good this morning."

How she wanted to tell him about her first encounter with Jack, how humiliated she'd felt. And now, how her heart ached. She wanted to puke it all out in a rush of words, but she fought to maintain control, even with Dad.

Between his tenderness and her hangover, maintaining control was near impossible. He took her hand and pulled her in closer so he could wrap his arms around her.

She remembered breaking her leg on the playground. Dad had scooped her up in his strong arms and carried her to the car for the trip to the hospital. As he'd lifted her, she thought she was higher than the trees, he was so tall. She'd wept against his shoulder then, pulling her strength from his. Now, his embrace was still strong, but he couldn't lift her from this. She had to do that herself.

"What is it, sweetie? What's had you tied up in knots with Jack? I've seen it from day one, and I was hoping all that tension was leading to a love match."

She sat up and smiled. "You watch too many reruns of *The Love Boat*. If only life were that easy. Sixty minutes to bliss." She watched a robin land on a branch outside the window. "Dad, it's so hard to explain. I don't even understand it all myself."

"Give it whirl."

She described the day she got the envelope with powder in it. Finally, as she talked, the stiffness she'd carried in her muscles since that day eased. She told him how exposed she'd felt when she'd seen her reflection, and how she'd hated whoever was behind the hazmat mask.

"Jack and I ... got close one night ..."

She caught the grin he stifled.

"and ... later, he said he wasn't a doctor, as I had believed, and that he was the hazmat guy, which I wasn't expecting at all. It blew me away, Dad. I felt as betrayed as ... as ..." She looked back at the robin, and it flew away.

He took her hand. "As betrayed as the day Mark left you at the altar. And as humiliated."

She nodded.

"I'm sorry you're hurting so bad, Sliver."

"Thanks, Dad." She tried to smile but probably grimaced.

"So, dancing with him, that was tough, huh? You hate him so much you didn't want to be near him let alone touch him. I can see where that would ruffle your feathers." He stared at the floor as he spoke, but something about the twitch of his mouth didn't match his words.

She heaved a sigh. "Yes." *Please stop, Dad.*

He nodded but continued to stare at the floor, saying nothing.

After a moment, she capitulated. "All right. Yes, I am attracted to him. Was. No, I didn't want to dance with him, but I didn't want to cause a scene at Isaiah's party." She closed her eyes, remembering the feel of Jack's arms around her, his breath soft near her ear. Her shoulders drooped, as if a heavy weight pressed them down, and her hands rested helplessly in her lap. The wall clock ticked into the silence, urging her.

She whispered, "Yes ... I guess I did want to dance with him ..." She stared at the same spot on the floor Dad was intent on. "Dad, I'm so confused."

"Sliver, you're in a tough spot. It's like wrangling with a huge trout. You've got him on the hook, but he's fighting like the devil. You can't land him, and you don't want to lose him. Your arms and back get tired, your legs get wobbly, and you risk falling into the cold river. You've got to decide what to do. Do you grab the net and try to bring him in? You and I know you probably can. Do you give it up and cut him loose? That way you won't risk falling in the cold river. But then you never know how good it could have been. And you'll never forget that one."

She let his words wash through her, closing her eyes and listening as if to a prayer. Maybe she was tired, maybe just hungover, but she was floating in that river. Like the sky and the water, her mind became crystal clear. She had been unfair. Jack had been there to help save her life.

"Jesus," she swore.

"Good idea, sweetie, say a prayer." He patted her shoulder.

"I may be too late, Dad."

JACK'S HEAD POUNDED. He pulled the pillow over his ears but that only made the noise echo loudly. Groaning, he opened his eyes and checked the clock. At first the digital numbers blurred into a red blob, but he blinked a couple times and they cleared. So did the sight of a lipstick tube on his nightstand.

Jerking up on his elbow, he lifted the sheets. Naked. Jack-hammers drilled in his head. He flopped back down. *Who the hell did I bring home?* The redhead. He squeezed his eyes shut and groaned inwardly. *Face it, man.* He rolled to his other side.

Empty. The bed was so rumpled, there could have been a ménage a trois the night before. Hell, there could have been an orgy in his bed. Checking out the pillow, he couldn't tell if her head had lain there all night ... or where it might have lain. *Shit.*

He threw back the covers and padded to the bathroom. No sign of her. *God, I hope she's not downstairs dressed in my bathrobe cooking breakfast.* But he didn't own a bathrobe and he didn't smell any food. Or coffee... She must have left during the night. He squinted at the sun assailing him from between the slats of the blinds. *Or at least before dawn.*

Back in the bedroom, he checked the clock again since the sight of the lipstick had blocked out the time. It was 9:30 a.m. He yawned. *Geez, my breath stinks.* He sniffed his armpit. *I stink.* He ran the shower and stood under the steamy hot water until it cooled. Casting his mind back to the night before, he tried to remember what happened. His clearest memory was the sight of Layla leaving the party. His chest tightened, and he clenched his jaw.

The hell with her. She wouldn't tell him what bug she had up her ass. He'd tried to apologize. Screw her. Time to move on. Hopefully, he'd gotten that redhead's number. What was her name again?

A GENTLE BREEZE teased the strands of hair that had escaped from Layla's ponytail, and the mid-morning sun warmed her cheeks. With the effect of a Zen fountain, the river gurgled over a branch stuck in the bank, calming her heart. She unzipped her vest, then her jacket beneath. She breathed deeply, savoring the serenity of the moment, but her shoulders were still tense with her feelings for Jack and her increasing thoughts of the stalker. As she often did now, she studied the area.

"What is it, sweetie? You've been looking over your shoulder all day."

Though Dad knew about the white powder incident, she

hadn't told him about the other threats. The last thing he needed was to worry about her. She shrugged.

"Just wondering who else is after the big fish." She gave him her most engaging smile.

"Uh-huh." He lowered his brows. Evidently giving up on finding out, he held his line in his left hand, and snapped his right wrist, casting downstream into the river, the tip of his rod down, following the fly. A circle of ripples surrounded the fly as it disappeared.

"You got one, Dad!"

He expertly pulled up on the rod and tugged on his line, setting the hook. Finally, he reeled in a trout that flailed and flapped in a valiant effort to escape.

Grabbing his net, he scooped in the fish. "Swallowed the hook." He unclipped the hemostat from the flap of his vest pocket while holding the fish belly up with his left hand. With his right, he took the scissor-like instrument and inserted it into the quiet trout's mouth. Gently, he dislodged the hook. He held up the fish. "He's a beauty!"

Layla had her phone ready and snapped his picture. "Good one, Dad."

He handed it to her, and she skimmed it below the surface of water until it recovered and wiggled. Then she released it.

She kissed Dad on his forehead and squeezed him. "Nice work."

He smiled at her, but his eyes looked tired.

"How about we head home?" She clipped the hemostat back on his vest.

"Whatever works for you." He smiled up at her. "Hey, could we stop on the way so I can pick up my prescription?"

"Sure, Dad."

As they packed up their gear, Layla realized how good for her this outing had been. She'd had moments when she hadn't been consumed with thoughts of Jack or the stalker. Now the aware-ness that the stalker could be anywhere returned, and all the peace she'd felt on the river dissipated.

"You okay, Sliver?" Dad reached out to take her hand.

"Yes. Just thinking about the one that got away." She smiled and kissed his cheek. *The fish or Jack? I need to call him and try to explain.* No, not needed to. Wanted to.

Dad scrutinized her, his mouth twitched to one side. She'd never been able to fool him.

She pushed his wheelchair up the ramp, glad for the opportu-nity to be out of his range of vision. "This has been a wonderful day, Dad."

"Sure has. Stay and have lunch with me."

"I'd love to." How long would she be able to deflect his ques-tions? Would she make it past the salad course?

As she stowed his wheelchair in the back and hit the button to close the hatch, she surreptitiously scanned the parking lot, searching for anyone who appeared out of place.

And there he was.

THIRTY

Jack's head was beginning to clear after his shower and a pot of strong, black coffee. He'd checked around his condo for a note, but there was no sign of the redhead's number. He scrolled through his phone looking for an unfamiliar contact, but to no avail.

The acrid aroma of burnt toast filled the kitchen. When the toast popped up, smoke coiled up from the blackened piece of bread.

"Perfect." Nothing helped an upset stomach better than burnt toast. That was one of the few good lessons he'd learned from his hungover father.

His head started pounding again. No, it was coming from his front door.

"Hang on! Hang on! I'm coming." *Please stop.*

Opening it, he ducked as Steve was ready to pound again. Jack grabbed his fist. "Don't even think about it."

Steve grinned, clearly enjoying his agony. "Quite a night you had there, Jack."

Jack led him to the kitchen and poured thick, dark coffee into a mug.

Steve sipped it and almost spit it out. "What is this? Mud?"

"I needed something strong." Jack tilted the slats of the blinds to block the morning sun. He crunched into the toast, sending black crumbs flying through the air.

"No doubt. What was that all about last night?"

"Wha' was wha' aw abou'?" Between the dry toast and his hangover, his mouth was as dry as the Sahara. Gripped by a coughing spell, he tried to clear his throat, then downed a hefty swig of coffee.

"You drank like a sailor—I've never seen you put that much away. And you were practically mauling Amber."

"Malt and amber? I mixed scotch with beer?"

Steve's eyes bugged out. "You idiot! Amber was the woman you were dancing with—practically copulating with—all night. You left together."

"Oh, so that's her name." At least it was a start.

Steve caught sight of the lipstick Jack had placed beside his phone as a reminder to look up her number. His eyebrows rose almost to his hairline, and he whistled. He picked up the tube and rotated it between his index finger and thumb. "Wow, Porsche, you were in high gear. You had a better night than I'd thought."

Jack grabbed the lipstick and slapped it back on the table, wincing at the sound. The case cracked. "Shit." He dropped his head in his hands.

"So ..." Steve leaned forward, hands clasped like a priest eager to hear a confession. "Give me details."

Instead Jack offered him a baleful stare.

After a minute, Steve sat back, draping one arm over the back of the chair. "You don't remember."

Jack's glared dissolved into confusion. "Not a goddamn thing.

She was gone when I woke up." He tossed the lipstick in the trash.

"If I know Amber, she'll be back. No worries."

"Oh, good." Jack rubbed his eyes, then scrubbed his hands through his hair.

"Try to contain your enthusiasm, Porsche. I've been trying to date her for months, and she just tumbles into your bed."

"Sorry, man. I didn't mean to...I really wanted... Shit." He rubbed his face again, scratching his beard. Layla's face close to his, her soft perfume scent, played in his mind. "Shit."

"Nice talk while you're eating your ...whatever you're eating." Steve got up and opened the refrigerator. "Got any eggs?"

Jack's stomach lurched and he ran to the bathroom. Several minutes later, gut aching from the effort, he returned to the kitchen, the smell of eggs and bacon almost too much to bear.

"You need to eat." Steve slid scrambled eggs on a plate and put it in front of Jack.

Jack's stomach gurgled and pitched.

"Obviously, the bacon is too much for you." He slid the slices onto his own plate and crunched the first one.

"So Amber was your surrogate." Steve wiped a greasy finger on his pant leg.

Jack gaped at him, trying to make sense of this.

"For Layla. She was your surrogate." Steve crunched another slice.

"What the hell are you talking about?" Jack gripped his head.

"Layla walked out on you, so ..."

Jack slammed a fist on the table, wincing against the sound and the resulting jiggling of the salt and pepper shakers. "You son of a—"

"Face it, Jack. That's what you did. Though I commend you for getting too drunk to be able to pull it off."

This time Jack wanted to slam his fist right into Steve's smug face. Somewhere deep inside, the ring of truth slithered up like the smoke from his black toast. "Just shut up, okay?" He took a bite of cold, rubbery scrambled eggs and gagged while it slid down his throat. "Maybe, just maybe, I was attracted to Amanda."

"Amber."

"Whatever. And maybe, just maybe, she was the woman I wanted to be with." His lie sat as cold and hard in his gut as the egg.

"And maybe the moon really is made of green cheese." Steve shoved the last piece of bacon into his mouth. "Face it, Trenton. You've been ensnared by a dark-haired beauty who has no time for you. If you are so interested in Amber, call her right now and ask her out tonight." He pushed Jack's phone toward him.

Amber, Amber. Jack scrolled through his contacts again, but no Amber appeared. He scratched his ear. "I guess I don't have her number."

"No joke. You didn't even have her name." Steve stabbed a piece of Jack's egg and ate it.

Jack gagged.

"So, if I give you her number, you'll call her right now and ask her out?"

Jack's stomach roiled. "You have her number?"

"Yes." He glared at Jack. "And it took me a long time to finally get it." He studied his phone. "I don't know why I'm doing this. I'm throwing her right at you. You should have to struggle like I did to get her contact info." His shoulders slumped. "Who am I kidding? I'm just a Corvair eating your dust."

"Geez, would you stop with that Covair and Porsche shit? Steve, you're a great guy ..."

"Don't romance me, Jack. You've got your hands full with a redhead and a brunette right now."

"I don't have a brunette." Jack clenched his fist ready to slam the table again but thought better of it.

"But you want her. So bad. So you had Amber instead. Don't deny it, Jack."

"That's harsh. I'm not that kind of guy." *Am I?*

"Not when you're sober. But last night you drank enough for an army—or at least a platoon. Sorry to break this to you, but you were a bastard last night."

"Give me her number. I'll call her right now. I don't use people."

Steve sent him Amber's number.

Just as Jack poised his finger above her number, the doorbell rang, its chimes on the wall right above his head. He squeezed his eyes shut and plugged his ears. Turning quickly to jump up and get the door, instead he headed for the bathroom for another round of detox. Above his vomiting, he heard Steve's voice.

"Oh, hi, Amber. We were just talking about you."

THIRTY-ONE

Hunched down with a hoodie pulled low on his forehead, a man sat in a charcoal gray sedan in the far corner of the parking lot. The shadow of the budding trees shifted, reflecting off the windshield and hiding his face. When he caught her looking at him, he slouched in the seat, looking down to hide his face.

Layla willed the SUV's hatch to close—did it always take this long? Jumping into the car, she started the engine, hit the accelerator, burning rubber, and sped out of the parking lot. An engine revved behind her.

"Layla, what the hell ...?"

"Just hold on tight, Dad."

She kept glancing in the rearview mirror, watching him swerve out of the parking lot, fishtailing along the drive.

"You need to tell me what's going on." Dad was more demanding than she'd heard since her teenage years.

"Not now, Dad."

She sped along the parkway, zigzagging between cars like a person she usually swore at. Taking the southbound entrance, she merged onto US 131 and drove like her life depended on it. Which it did. Hers and Dad's.

Her stalker entered the highway and stayed a car length behind her, letting another car get in between them.

Myriad possibilities ran through her mind. She was too far from downtown to drive to the police station. She didn't want to lead him to Brookside, and she didn't want to lead him to her house. Where should she go?

Reaching for her purse, she pulled out her phone and hit a button. "Call 911." Her hand trembled so she almost dropped her phone.

"Layla, what the hell—?" Dad snapped.

"911. What is your emergency?" The operator was unemotional, almost robotic.

"I'm being chased by a man who has been stalking me."

"What is your location?" If the monotone voice was meant to calm her, it had the opposite result. *Come on, get excited here, our lives are on the line!*

She glanced at the sign on the overpass ahead. "I'm on 131 at the exit for 196."

"Which way are you heading on 131, ma'am?" She might as well have been asking "How's the weather in your part of town?" The calmer the dispatcher sounded, the more livid Layla got.

The next exit was the one she normally took to Dad's. She sped by it. The car behind her took it, leaving the stalker right behind her.

"What the hell ...?" Dad was checking the side-view mirror. "Who is this stalker?"

"Long story."

"Excuse me? Repeat that direction," the operator droned.

"South." She looked from the rearview mirror to the road and back again as she sped along. Her mind raced faster than the car. She had to lose this guy. The next exit loomed ahead. She drove as if she would pass it, then careened onto it at the last minute, leaving the stalker no choice but to continue down the highway. Another driver who had turned on the exit laid on his horn.

She waved apologetically to the fuming driver.

"Are you still there?" the monotone voice asked.

"Yes. I'm heading east on Wealthy Street and turning north on Division."

"There's a patrol car in that vicinity."

"I'll wait for him at the pharmacy on the corner of Fulton and Elmgrove."

"What is the make and model of your car?"

"I'm in a brown Suburban. I don't know what year it is. Old. It's old."

"His ETA is five minutes."

Resuming a normal speed, she finally took a breath. Her heart pumped, threatening to break a rib. Now shaking, she eased down the road, checking her rearview mirror repeatedly.

The stalker was nowhere in sight.

"It's time you told me what this is all about." Dad was glaring at her.

"There have been a couple more incidents since the powder." Though she tried to stop it, her voice trembled as she spoke. "Someone is stalking me, and he was in the parking lot. I had to get away from him."

"Why haven't you told me about this?" Dad's bellow rang around the interior.

"I didn't want to worry you."

"Didn't want to worry me?" He sputtered, unable to continue.

"Dad, give me a minute to calm down. Let's talk about this back at your place, okay?"

"No! I'm going to talk about it now. Look, I'm not some baby you need to mollycoddle. I'm your father. My body may not be what it was, but my mind is strong and my love for you is stronger. You have to stop treating me like some old fart with one foot in the grave. I'm your goddamn father. Treat me with some respect!"

She gripped the wheel as if it were a lifeline. If she let go, she would spin out of control. She'd never meant to cause her father to feel diminished, and yet, that was how she'd been treating him.

"Dad, just let me get you home."

She had doubled back toward Brookside and was driving along Fulton Street to the pharmacy.

Right at the end of Jack's street.

How much more could she take?

She pulled into the parking lot and backed into a spot right in front of the door but facing the road so she could watch for the patrol car. She took advantage of the handicap tag when Dad was in the car. "Look, I'm going to run in, get your prescription, then we'll head home, and I'll explain what's going on, okay?" She turned off the engine. She looked in Dad's eyes, and his pain broke her heart. She put her hand on his. "I'm sorry, Dad. I thought I was doing the right thing. I was wrong."

He gave her a half smile. "We'll straighten all this out, Sliver."

She laughed and kissed his cheek. "We will."

The store was deserted, save for the tall, scrawny kid behind the counter. As she paid for the prescription, her car engine started. Looking out the window, she screamed, "No!" as her SUV drove off.

THIRTY-TWO

Jack would rather have stayed in the bathroom vomiting than face Amanda...no, Amber. He gripped the sink edge and squeezed his eyes shut, trying to call up a memory, an image, anything from last night. Had he slept with her? Had he not been able to get it up? He groaned. The outcome of last night determined how he greeted her this morning. If he'd slept with her, he didn't want to come off as a douche. If he hadn't been able to ... he didn't want to look like a fool.

No matter how tightly he gripped the sink or squeezed his eyes, no memory came to him.

"Jack's not feeling so well this morning." Steve sounded contrite, as if he'd been the fool who drank too much.

Amber laughed—no, giggled.

Jesus, help me.

"No wonder. He had quite a workout last night." She giggled again.

Steve was silent.

Jack stared in the mirror. His pale face, scruffy beard, and dull eyes made him look like one of PJ's druggies. *Time to face the music, Trenton.* He splashed cold water on his face and took a swig of mouthwash, swishing and spitting it out.

"Morning." It sounded more like a croak. He cleared his throat.

She rose from the kitchen table, leading with her breasts and pulling her tight skirt down as she straightened.

Steve remained seated, looking as if he would faint.

Her musky perfume wafted to Jack, and his stomach lurched. He lingered near the bathroom door.

But she was nothing if not determined. She sashayed to him, planting a kiss on his cheek. The cloud of musk overpowered him.

"'Scuse me." He bolted into the bathroom, shutting the door. Another round of retching left him sprawled on the bathroom floor, its cold tile somehow comforting. Pulling himself up by the bathtub rim, he grabbed his toothbrush and scrubbed his teeth until his gums yelled, *stop!* He took another swig of mouthwash and swished until the burning was unbearable. After spitting it out, he took three long, deep breaths.

Though he'd earlier run the hot water cold, he longed for another shower.

Swiping a comb through his hair, he splashed his face again and faced the door. *No more delays, Trenton. Just get out there.*

Steve was brewing a fresh pot of coffee, and the aroma helped to tamp down the musk. She sat at the table like a puppy waiting at the door for the owner's return, bright-eyed, big smile. If she'd had a tail, it would be wagging.

"Sorry about that, er, Aman-"

"Amber," Steve pronounced her name loudly and clearly, throwing dagger eyes at him over her head. "said she completely understands, after the night you two had."

She smiled at him conspiratorially. "Yes, Jackie, I completely understand." She wiggled her shoulders back and forth.

Behind Amber, Steve mouthed *Jackie?* And laughed silently as he held his stomach.

Jack couldn't glare at him with her watching his every facial expression.

"Well, I need to get to the station. I'll leave you two lovebirds to yourselves."

Jack growled.

"Ooooh!" Amber now sounded like Betty Boop.

Jesus, help me.

"No, hang out and have coffee with us, Steve. You're not on today, are you?"

"I want to stop by and, uh, see how things are going there." Steve looked down at Amber. "Bye, Amber."

She gave him a cursory glance and turned her attention to Jack. "Bye, Steve."

Steve's disappointed green eyes popped another puppy dog analogy into Jack's mind. He shook his head. *Sorry, Steve. I didn't ask for this.*

Hell, maybe I did.

When the door closed behind Steve, Amber rose and slunk to Jack. He supposed this was supposed to be sexy, but he thought of Gollum creeping up to Frodo.

She caressed his cheek and ran a finger along his jawline. "How are you feeling today, baby?"

Oh, geez. But if Layla had approached him like that? Called him baby? Caressed his cheek? The last thing he'd be thinking about would be Gollum. He had to stop comparing Layla to every other woman he might encounter.

Good luck with that.

"I'm okay. Coffee helped."

"You were pretty out of it last night." She moved closer, pressing her breasts into his chest. Her arms went up around his shoulders.

Like it or not, his body reacted.

"I thought we could pick up where we left off." She brushed her lips along his.

Where we left off! He could find out just where that was. "Where exactly was that?" He didn't pull away.

She kissed along his jawline, back to his mouth, and pressed against him as she kissed him, thrusting her tongue into his mouth. She slid her arms along his back, resting them on his butt.

"Does it matter? We can just start again."

He pulled back. "Just tell me what we did." He stopped. *Way to screw this up, Trenton.* He pulled her hands away from his butt and held them in his. "I mean, why don't you describe it to me so I know what territory I didn't cover."

She dropped her arms. "You don't remember, do you?" Her eyes narrowed, then softened. "Well, you were drinking pretty hard." She tilted her head and looked up at him out of the corner of her eye, a sly smile. "I know. We'll play 'strip tell-what-happened-last-night.' Every time I tell you what you did to me, you have to take something off. Every time you tell me what I did to you, I have to take something off."

Jack had to admit it was an intriguing game. If only he were playing it with Layla. "What if I don't remember what I did to you?"

She giggled. "Then I guess you'll be standing here naked, and I'll have the better view." She slid her hands along his chest to his waist. "And I can have my way with you." She licked her lips.

"Why don't you just tell me what happened?"

"What fun would that be, Jackie?"

His stomach lurched.

LAYLA STOOD, hands on hips, leaning into the face of a young cop. The red lights atop his car flashed in a dizzying circle.

"What do you mean you can't take me with you? He's got my father."

"Ma'am, civilians can't ride along when we're chasing a perpetrator. You just stay here, and we'll let you know when we find him."

He may as well have patted her head and called her "little lady." She swallowed back the urge to make his youthful face less handsome. "Please, Dad is in that car."

He opened the patrol car door and slid in, calling back, "Then the faster I get to it, the better." He sped off.

Layla's insides were serpents tangled together looking for a way out. She had to get to Dad. Her cell phone was in her purse, in the car. She looked back at the pharmacy, then down the street. Down the street where Jack lived. Could she even remember which condo was his?

The serpents slithered, sending her running in a blind panic toward his place. Running along the street, she tried to read the numbers. Then she remembered—there was a beautiful maple tree in front of his unit. She spotted it, ran up the steps to the door, and stopped.

This is no time for junior high crush jitters. Ring the bell. Ring the damn bell.

She jabbed the doorbell, heart racing. *Please be home.*

Jack opened the door. Her knees trembled so, she buckled. The words she never wanted to say, never wanted to have to say, bubbled up and tumbled out.

"Jack, I need you." She collapsed into his arms.

"Layla." His whisper was like a prayer, his arms like a refuge. She pulled him close.

"Jackie?"

Her heart dropped. Behind Jack, the redhead appeared,

coming in from the kitchen. Then she noticed the lipstick along his jaw and smeared on his lips.

She stepped back. "Oh." That's all she could manage to say. The snakes twisted inside her, hissing "foolish" at her. She stepped back through the door, but Jack grabbed her arm and pulled her in.

"What is it? What's happened?"

She tore her eyes away from the redhead. She didn't matter, he didn't matter. Only Dad mattered. She grabbed his arms. "He's got Dad."

"Who?"

She choked out a gasp.

"Oh, my God. Your stalker?"

"What's going on, Jackie?" The redhead came up and tried to wrap her arm through his.

He disengaged her arm, his eyes never leaving Layla.

Finally, he looked back at her. "Amanda, I've got to go."

"Amber." She pouted.

"Sorry." He headed toward the kitchen table, grabbing his wallet and keys.

"I can wait here for you ..."

He picked up her purse from the end table and shoved it at her. "No." He hustled her out the front door.

"Call me," she called back.

Layla leaned against the doorjamb, her legs still trembling. Jack pulled her to him, supporting her as they left the condo.

"It's okay, Layla, we'll find him. He's going to be all right."

She nodded and hiccupped back a sob.

"Which direction did he take?" He careened down the street, following the directions she pointed in, screeching onto the main drag. "He's in your car?"

"Yes." She fought to get the words out.

Suddenly, the police radio in his truck squawked. "Accident

on US 131 near the Franklin Street exit. Brown SUV, crashed into the guardrail."

Another voice. "Copy. I'm at Wealthy and 131. Responding now."

Layla's heart thumped. That was Dad. "Dear God, somehow, let him be okay."

Jack took her hand. He activated the emergency lights on his truck and stepped on the gas. The truck lurched forward. He sped over to Cherry Street, slid onto the entrance to US 131, and flew down the ramp. Cars pulled out of his way, and he zigzagged through the traffic that didn't bother.

Layla gripped his hand and with her other, held onto the armrest on the door to keep her balance. Cars slowed and crowded the lanes. Jack pulled to the shoulder and they bounced along. Up ahead she spotted her car, the front end smashed against the guardrail.

"Oh my God, there he is."

Jack skidded to a stop in front of the SUV. They both jumped out, and while Jack paused at the back door of his truck, she ran toward the vehicle. Layla could see spidery cracks emanating from a central hole on the passenger-side window.

"Dad." Her strangled cry was lost in the noise of beeping horns and crawling traffic. In the distance a siren dopplered through the air.

She reached the passenger door at the same time Jack did. He pushed her aside.

"Let me check before you see him." His gentle look said what he couldn't. Dad might be badly injured, a gory sight. Dad might be dead.

She pushed forward. "No, I need to see him."

Jack pressed his lips together, nodded, and opened the door.

Dad's body had collapsed against the airbag, his face toward the driver. His right arm dangled loosely, and blood ran down his face, pooling in his ear. On the floor below his hand lay his hemostat.

Jack ran his hands along Dad's neck, spine and pelvis.

"Is he breathing? Is he ...?"

"Here, let me through." A rough hand grabbed her shoulder and yanked her away.

"Hey! This is my father!" She turned to face the young patrol cop who'd denied her a ride.

"How the hell did you get here so fast?" He tilted his hat back on his head.

Jack stood and leaned into him. "Shut up and help me get him out of here."

The cop glared at him.

"I'm an EMT. Now help me!"

Together the two men lifted Dad from the truck and laid him on the grassy shoulder. His flat eyes stared at the leaden sky as one breath escaped his slack mouth. Jack pressed an ear to his chest, then checked his pupils. He looked up at her. He didn't have to speak.

Dad was dead.

"No!" She crumpled beside him, taking Dad's face into her hands. "Please, don't leave me, Dad." Like waves, the sobs wracked her body as she continued to beg. This was complete. Mom had left her. Mark had left her. Now Dad. She ground her teeth and dug her hands into her stomach to stop the enormous screw that kept turning and driving into her. *God, how can you be so cruel? How can you take the one person who has stayed? I have no one else.*

THIRTY-THREE

Jack gently eased her back. "Layla, let me try." He checked Clarence's airways, then immediately began CPR, pressing his hands against Clarence's chest, pumping while he counted. After thirty, he puffed rescue breaths into Clarence's mouth, then pumped again.

Layla knelt beside him, counting for him. She patted Dad's arm, whispering prayers. Scattered through her counting, she made bargains with God, begging for Dad's life. "I'll be kinder. I'll be more loving. I promise." Tears streamed down her face. "Please, Dad. Please don't leave me. Not yet. Please!"

"Come on, Clarence. Come on back." Jack pumped, then breathed. Sweat dripped down his face as he continued the procedure. "Come on, Clarence. Damn it all, Dad. Don't give up!"

Layla jerked up to look at him.

He wiped his sleeve across his face but didn't look at her. "Keep counting," he croaked. He realized what he'd said. He was sixteen again, impotently pumping on his father's chest with his broken arm and dislocated shoulder. Cursing at him, praying for him, just as Layla prayed now.

His arms trembled, but when the cop tried to relieve him, he shoved him away like a man possessed. A drop of sweat bobbled on the tip of his nose, threatening to drop, holding its ground. His teeth ground with his effort; his jaw clenched like a trap. It was as if he were fighting for his own life.

He kept pumping, breathing, and yelling "come on" at Clarence.

Clarence coughed. He breathed. "Stop." Though his command was thready and weak, to Jack it was as if he'd shouted.

"Dad! Dad, it's me." Layla bent forward and clutched his hand.

She sobbed, searching Jack's eyes.. He sat back on his haunches, breathing hard. He grinned at her. He pressed his fingers against Clarence's throat and nodded. She reached out to him, clasping his hand, "Thank you."

An ambulance screeched to a halt behind his truck, and the attendants jumped out.

"I've got a pulse and heartbeat, but he needs transport now," Jack called to them.

They grabbed a gurney out of the back and wheeled it to him. Together, they lifted Clarence onto the stretcher and began checking his vital signs. One attendant hooked up an IV.

Layla helped Jack to stand, and he draped an arm around her shoulders, breathing heavily. "Thanks," he said between breaths. He smiled at her. "I think he's got a fighting chance."

Her breath hitched, and she choked out a sound somewhere between a guffaw and a croak. "Thanks to you. Thank you for saving Dad."

He squeezed her shoulder and kissed her forehead.

As if on cue, all the activity around them came into focus.

The crowd that had gathered, myriad vehicles with flashing lights and crackling radios.

The young cop pushed his way in and stuck his face in Clarence's. "Did you see who did this?" His strident voice carried over the EMTs who were trying to coordinate critical care.

"Did you see who kidnapped you?" he shouted as Clarence were deaf.

Jack pulled him away. "What the hell are you doing?"

"Getting a report. Move back, buddy." He hitched his belt.

"Why don't you let the first responders do their job so he can live to give a report?"

The cop glared at him, then turned away.

Layla supported Jack as they walked to his truck, halted, and looked back at the SUV.

"Jack, did you see anyone else in my car?"

"No, I was focused on Clarence."

"Me too."

She called out to the patrol cop. "Excuse me, officer." He either didn't hear her or ignored her. She wavered between helping Jack to the truck or approaching the cop.

Jack put his thumb and finger in the corners of his mouth and let out a shrill whistle.

The cop spun around, scowling, ready to arrest whoever whistled. His frown deepened as he approached. "Yeah? What do you need?" He glared at Jack.

"What about the other guy in the car?"

The cop shook his head. "No other guy."

Layla's heart thrummed. "That means the stalker's still out there."

"Any sign of the driver's injury?" Jack asked.

"Nothing major. The guy walked away from this."

"Thanks." Jack rubbed his right shoulder. But this time the pain was different. He counted this a win for sure.

He caught the look from the EMTs.

"Your dad is ready to be transported."

When they reached the ambulance, Clarence's eyes were closed, and his mouth was a straight line as he fought the pain of being moved.

"Dad, you're going to be all right." Layla's voice was tight.

"You betcha." His eyes fluttered open, trying to focus on her. He attempted a smile.

"You ride with him, and I'll stay to give a report. I'll meet you later at Mercy," Jack whispered against her ear. "I'll be there soon. I won't leave you."

Despite her fear, her eyes lit up. She believed him.

THIRTY-FOUR

Dr. Chandra entered Dad's room shortly after she and Jack were allowed in. His grave face told her that Dad's injuries were serious. He shook her hand, then Jack's before examining Dad.

"Your father is a fighter." He looked at Jack. "I hear you did a fine job with CPR. You saved his life."

Jack nodded his thanks.

The doctor turned to Layla. "There doesn't appear to be any internal bleeding. He suffered a concussion and two broken ribs. Because of his muscular sclerosis, we have to be extra vigilant. He's not out of the woods yet, but we'll do some more tests once he stabilizes."

"Thanks, Doctor." Layla was relieved, but still not peaceful. It was still touch and go.

She held Dad's hand, staring at his pale, drawn face, willing the next labored breath, willing him to live. He was her life, her center, her strength. But she heard his words.

I can't be everything to you, Sliver. You need to live your life for you. Surround yourself with friends, with fun, with love. You'll shrivel up and die if you keep isolating yourself. Be curious, be loving, be passionate.

When Mom died, Dad had been her rock, her savior, carrying her through grief she was incapable of carrying herself at such a young age. He'd guided her through life as best he could. But he never, ever, encouraged her to isolate herself. Their life had been full of friends and family, fun and adventure.

If Dad dies, what will my life be? What will I live for? She closed her eyes against the crush of loneliness that gripped her.

Every decision she'd made in the last few years since Dad's health declined had been for him. Or had it? Did she accept her promotion just to earn enough to keep Dad at Brookside? Or did it offer her the chance to become a workaholic, so she'd have no room in her life for others?

Had he been her crutch so she could avoid people who reminded her of her humiliation on what was supposed to be her wedding day? If she focused on Dad, she could crawl into her shell of a life and avoid people. Avoid vulnerability.

Hearing Jack move, she opened her eyes. He stood and checked Dad's vitals, the green light of the monitor glowing on his weary face. Dark circles showed below his eyes, and there was no sign of tempting dimples around his mouth, held taut in concentration.

She had known she loved him before today. She knew at Isaiah's party. She knew when they'd made love. She probably knew at the river when she'd been so mad that he took Dad fly fishing. She knew every time she'd heard his name and a tingle of pleasure ran along her skin. Or when he gave those annoying smirks that started heat in her middle and spread through her body.

But in this moment, even knowing that he could leave at any time, she loved him most. She knew it was worth the risk. He was worth the risk.

THE DIM LIGHTS, the pungent smells, and the hushed conversation gave the hospital room a sense of sacramental vigil. Jack checked the monitors, concerned by the numbers. With an oxygen saturation rate of 68 percent and blood pressure hovering around 70/40, Clarence was in a battle for his life. At least he had a battle. *Unlike my dad.*

Jack's gaze now shifted to Layla, sitting close to the head of the hospital bed, her hand clutching Clarence's, her eyes never leaving his face. He rose quietly and left the room, searching for a coffee machine. A nurse directed him to a lounge a few doors down.

Filling two cups, he stared at the neatly stacked packets of cream and sugar. He didn't know how Layla took her coffee. He grunted. How weird that he didn't know. He wanted to know exactly that. How she took her coffee, how she looked in the morning, if she slept on her back or side or stomach. What her favorite color was, what her favorite movie was, how she liked her eggs.

He hurried to the room with a handful of every kind of sweetener available and plenty of packets of creamer.

She turned to him as he entered, her expression confused, as if she weren't aware of her surroundings. She smiled her thanks as she took the cup, holding his gaze as she placed her hand on his arm.

"Thank you," she whispered. "Thank you for saving Dad's life."

His throat was thick, and he tried to clear it. Words wouldn't work right then, so he just smiled. He set her coffee on the rolling tray alongside the bed, depositing all the packets beside it.

She looked up at him, bemused.

"I didn't know how you took your coffee."

She laughed, a light musical laugh that echoed right around his heart. He pulled his chair closer to her on the pretense of needing a packet. He took his coffee black. But he took a sugar packet, flicked it, and poured it into his coffee. He took a sip and gagged.

"Are you all right?" Layla's eyes widened.

He nodded, setting his cup aside.

She took his hand again. "Jack, I owe you an apology."

He squeezed her hand, noticing how soft it was, how it cupped perfectly into his.

She turned in her chair, facing him square on. Strands of hair tumbled around her face, and black smudges streaked beneath her eyes. The tip of her nose was pink. But her eyes were soft, the lights of the machine highlighting the gold flecks against the dark brown color. She fascinated him, and he could have stared at her all day.

He brushed a strand of hair back from her forehead, then traced his finger along her cheek. "No apology necessary."

"But I need to explain—" A crease appeared between her brows.

He pressed a finger against her lips. "Not now. Let's talk things through later. You have enough to deal with right now with your dad."

They both looked at Clarence, who struggled with each breath despite the oxygen he was receiving.

"You called him Dad. While you were working on him, you said, 'Damn it all, Dad. Don't give up.'"

He said nothing.

He rubbed his temples. He'd been driven, working on Clarence without a pause, like a robot, like his own life had depended on Clarence surviving. And it had. At least his mental well-being. He was working on his own father again, but not as the slender, young sixteen-year-old. This time he could save him.

"Can you tell me about it?" Layla whispered.

"Yes." He stared at Clarence. "But not now."

The night shift nurse came in. She checked his vitals, then injected something into his IV.

"You two may as well go home and go to bed. He won't wake up until morning now." She smiled at them and bustled out.

"C'mon. I'll take you home." Jack picked up their jackets from the back of his chair.

She didn't let go of Clarence's hand. "I want to stay."

"You'll be more help to him tomorrow when he wakes up if you get some sleep tonight."

She sat still for a moment, then nodded. As she rose, she kissed Clarence's forehead. "Goodnight, Dad. I love you."

When she turned, she met Jack's gaze. "As I recall, you said you wouldn't leave me."

THIRTY-FIVE

Sunday, May 24

The Seth Thomas clock on the wall between the front windows read just after midnight when Layla flipped on the living room light. Her bones were tired, and her body ached. She rubbed her eyes.

Jack hovered by the door, his hands in his pockets.

She pulled him in and closed the door. "The nurse said we should go home and go to bed."

His grin was lopsided. "To get some rest."

She nodded, not wanting to break their gaze. Not wanting to move away from him. Certainly not wanting him to leave.

She rested her hands on his chest. She needed ... what? To not be alone. To continue sharing this day with him. To be with him. *Say it, Layla. Say it out loud.* But the words were weighty, and what she wanted to say wouldn't move up from her heart to her voice. *He promised he wouldn't leave you. He promised.* But others had promised, and they had left.

He kissed her forehead. "I'm here for you, Layla. For as long as you need. For whatever you need."

The words bubbled up; she couldn't have stopped them if she'd tried. "I need you, Jack. Will you stay? Will you just hold me?"

His arms wrapped around her. "Whatever you need. I'm here for you."

She was falling. She was flying. She was safe.

Taking his hand, she led him to the bedroom.

A nightlight glowed on the wall alongside her bed. In the misty light, he smiled at her.

"Why don't I run a hot bath for you?"

Her eyebrows shot up.

He held up his hands. "Just for you ... this time." He winked.

As wonderful as it sounded, she was too tired to wait for the tub to fill.

"A shower. It's quicker."

He nodded and headed to the bathroom.

After turning on the bedside lamp, she grabbed a pair of shorts and a T-shirt, then headed into the bathroom. He had his hand under the shower spray to test the water. "How hot do you like it?"

She unbuttoned her shirt and dropped it to the floor. "However you do."

LAYLA AWOKE; it was still dark. She lay spooned against Jack, just as they had fallen asleep. His breath was warm against her neck, his breathing soft and even. His arm lay across her breasts, cupping her shoulder. She wanted to snuggle even closer but didn't want to wake him. She dozed off.

When she awoke again, the early morning sun slanted through the blinds. She pulled the blankets tighter—Jack was gone. Her heart dropped to her stomach.

See? He left you. You're a fool. Everyone leaves you. She squeezed her eyes shut. *No. Not Jack. He promised.* She crushed the pillow around her head, trying to block the voice out.

A corner of the pillow lifted, and one eye peered in at her. "Cream, right? I found this hazelnut stuff."

She let the pillow fall away. Jack sat beside her with a steaming mug of coffee.

"I watched you at the hospital. You take your coffee with cream."

His hair stood up on one side of his head—the side he'd slept on. His scruffy beard couldn't hide his dimples as he gave his crooked grin. God, she loved him, and that knowledge surged through her.

"Yes. Cream. Thank you." She sat up letting the blanket fall away.

To his credit, his gaze didn't leave hers—at least not immediately. Then he slowly lowered it to her neck, her shoulders, and finally, her breasts. "You make me crazy."

She chuckled. "As you do me." She caressed his stubbly jawline.

"If you keep that up, we won't get to the hospital until lunch time." He kissed her softly and quickly rose. "I am only so strong, Ms. Forrester."

She pulled the blankets up and took a long sip of coffee. "I'm ready to go right now."

"First, sustenance. You need energy to help your dad get strong."

LAYLA HELD DAD'S HAND, watching his eyelids flicker in dreams, cherishing the beep, beep, beep that announced his steady heartbeat, relishing the warmth of his hand in hers. His breathing wasn't as labored this morning. *Thank you, God. Thank you, God.* She'd repeated this prayer a thousand times in the last twelve hours.

The cocoon of the hospital room wrapped them in quiet, disturbed only by the rhythmic sound of monitors and muted conversations in the hall. Just the dim light above Dad's head lit the room, wrapping them in a twilight watch.

Pulling her focus from Dad, she smiled at Jack who sat in the easy chair in the shadowy corner. He still hadn't shaved and his five o'clock shadow had deepened into stubble that stood dark against his white teeth when he smiled back. She understood the Grinch when his heart grew three sizes; only hers had grown at least ten and was glowing and warm within her.

A squeeze of her hand. Her gaze flew back to Dad, who was peering at her from the corners of his eyes.

"Dad."

He blinked, and one corner of his mouth hitched up just enough for her to see it.

"Oh, Dad." She leaned in and kissed his forehead.

He squeezed her hand again. His lips moved but emitted no sound.

"Shh. Save your strength for healing." She pulled the covers up higher on his chest.

The morning nurse breezed in. "Good morning, Clarence. Are you going to stay awake for me this time?" Layla resisted covering her ears against the nurse's strident voice. No wonder people couldn't sleep in the hospital.

The woman bustled about, checking his vital signs and refreshing the IV. When she finished, she smiled at Layla. "We've been cutting back on the morphine, so he should be more alert as the day progresses."

"Mmmph," Dad whispered.

"Shh, Dad ..."

The nurse wrote on the chart. "No, let him talk. The more he tries, the quicker his speech will become understandable."

"Tha...mmmph," Dad said, nodding just a bit.

"You're welcome, Clarence." She patted his hand. "I'll be back," she called as she left.

Jack stood next to Layla, placing his hand on her shoulder.

Dad's eyebrows raised, and he nodded harder. "Ye ... goo."

He looked from Layla to Jack and back. Was that a twinkle in his eyes?

"I'll go get us some coffee." Jack kissed the top of her head.

Dad's eyes crinkled, and he winked at her. "Fine ... ally." His eyes closed.

When Jack returned, he stood by Dad's bed and took his hand. How long had it been since joy had bloomed within her like this? Far, far too long.

"You're a stubborn old coot." Jack grinned at him.

Dad managed a half grin, then sobered. "You ... saved ...my... life." He took a deep breath. "I ... was dead."

"You promised to show me your favorite fishing spot. You can't get out of it that easily."

Dad gave him a full grin, then closed his eyes.

THIRTY-SIX

Monday, May 25

The *click, click, click* of her Jimmy Choos was slower than usual as Layla walked the gauntlet at noon the next day. She didn't keep her gaze averted but responded to the paralegals' greetings as she passed. She recognized curiosity or sympathy in their eyes, but not hostility.

Angela met her, empty-handed, at the door of her office. "I'll get you some coffee," she said.

Layla nodded. "Thanks, Angela. That would be great."

"Hazelnut, right?"

Layla smiled. "Yes, please."

The buzz of the overhead light welcomed her in, but she turned it off and switched on her desk lamp. After a morning spent with the constant noise of hospital monitors and police station bustle, she needed quiet.

She and Jack had gotten to the hospital before dawn and spent several hours with Dad, thrilled at the progress he was making in just a couple of days.

Dad was exhausted after the morning routine of doctor's

call, vital-signs checks, tests, breakfast, and meds. The nurse gave him a sleeping pill, and once he'd drifted off, Layla left for the office, leaving strict instructions that she be called when he awoke.

Before she came to the office, she'd met Isaiah at the police station to finalize the accident report. So far, they had no leads on the stalker. No prints in the car. Nothing left behind to identify him.

She rubbed her eyes and fired up her computer.

Angela returned with a steaming mug of coffee and a choco-late-covered doughnut. "Just in case you need energy." She smiled, but her eyes were guarded.

"Thank you, Angela. Thanks for everything."

Angela's eyes brightened. "You're welcome, Ms. Forrester. Sorry about your father's accident. Is he okay?"

"He's doing pretty well, but it will take time. Thanks."

Angela nodded and left.

Layla pulled up a case file and read the first sentence.

"You gonna order me to lunch again today?" Mariana leaned against the doorjamb.

Layla grinned. "Was that how it sounded?"

Mariana sat, folding her hands on the desk. "Yeah, pretty much. But I didn't mind. I knew you'd come around. How's your father?"

"He's doing well—better than expected. I spent the morning with him."

"Good to hear. You look pretty tired. Why not take this after-noon off and rest?"

Layla ran her fingers through her hair. "I can't. I'm going to work this afternoon, join Dad and Jack for a delicious hospital dinner, and come back and work later tonight."

Mariana tilted her head, cascading silken black hair over one shoulder. "Well, you wouldn't want to be rested so you can help him heal. I mean, why take a nap when you can save the world here?"

Layla fought down her usual caustic retort. *Mariana is being a friend. She cares about me. And that's okay.*

"Okay. I'll work this afternoon because I'm too wound up to sleep right now. And I'll reconsider coming in tonight. Deal?"

"Deal." Mariana extended her hand, and Layla shook it, amazed at how good it felt. Connecting with someone ... with a friend. Mariana smiled at her. "And I want to hear more about this Jack. Later."

Layla turned to her computer and opened her calendar. There was something she needed to do when Dad was stable, and she wasn't so tired. She clicked on tomorrow's date and typed in a reminder.

Call Connie.

"Hi, Miss Forrester." Jimmy grinned from her office door. His shirt and pants were clean though not ironed. His bowtie was missing.

"Hey, Jimmy." His smile was a soothing balm. "How're the Tigers doing?"

"They lost to Milwaukee last night." He hustled to her desk and set down her mail in its usual place.

His smile vanished. "I ... I'm sorry about your dad's accident. How is he doing?"

How does he know about that? "Thank you, Jimmy. He's doing better." She cocked her head. "How did you hear about his accident?"

"Trevor told me."

Her blood turned icy. She fought the fear fluttering in her gut and tried to sound casual. "How is Trevor doing?"

"He's good. He got a new job."

"Oh? That's good."

"Yeah, he works here now." He stood taller and grinned broadly.

"Here?" Every drop of moisture had evaporated from her mouth.

He nodded. "Yes! He's a cus...custodian."

The room swam before her eyes.

THIRTY-SEVEN

Jack chewed the last of his Salisbury steak. And chewed. And chewed. Layla grinned, spooning up mashed potatoes the consistency of thick pea soup. Her smile couldn't hide the exhaustion on her face. The bright smile she bestowed on Clarence didn't fool her father either.

"So, Clarence, what happened to cause the accident?" Jack finally swallowed the mystery meat.

"That guy drove like a maniac. I figured he was going to kill me anyway, so I decided to take him with me. As he was speeding along 131, I grabbed my hemostat and aimed for his eye, but he must have seen me move, so he held up his arm. I jabbed him really hard in his upper arm and snatched the steering wheel."

He closed his eyes and rested for a minute then opened them and continued.

"We went a-flying." He closed his eyes and coughed.

Jack glanced at the monitors. Heartbeat steady, blood pressure 94/62, pulse 90. Clarence was exhausted, but he was in stable condition.

Layla held Clarence's Styrofoam cup of ice water, tilting the straw so he could drink. After she put it back on the table, she leaned toward him, her body tensed, her fists clenched, as if ready to ward off a physical attack.

"Dad, did you see who it was?"

Clarence's eyes darkened. "No. The police asked me that, too. Wait! He had a hood on..." He squeezed his eyes closed. "I'm sorry, Sliver." He wiped his forehead. "I mean I probably did, but I can't remember anything else." He closed his eyes again for a moment, concentrating. He opened them, shook his head, and grasped her hand. "Just like I told that detective, I'm sorry I can't be of more help."

She smiled and fussed with his blanket. Jack could see the disappointment in her eyes.

"Not a problem, Dad. The police will find him."

"Layla, go home and get some rest. I'll be here tomorrow—I'm not going anywhere." He held her hand.

A nurse entered rolling in a computer cart. "Good evening, Clarence. I'm going to take your vitals and then send you off to dreamland." She smiled at Layla. "He'll be out for the night, so you two may as well go home and get some sleep, too."

"See? She's kicking you out."

"Okay, Dad. She rose and kissed his forehead. "I'll see you in the morning."

"Yeah but let me sleep in a little. Don't get here before the sun comes up." He winked at Jack.

Jack thought of a good way to keep her occupied in the morning.

As they made their way through the parking garage, Layla fished out her keys for the rental car then handed her own keyring to him, holding one up. "Here's the key to my condo. I need to run into the office, and then I'll meet you back there."

Jack halted and looked at her. "It's late, and you've been going full steam for two days. Come back with me, and I'll make us omelets that will erase the taste of whatever we just ate."

She hesitated. "I'd like that. Listen, I won't stay and work like I'd planned. I'll just pick up my laptop and come right home."

Home. That word had never affected him like this. It had always simply meant where he went to sleep and shower. But when she said it, he got this weird, warm sensation that he relished. The two of them together, no matter where they were, would be home. He liked the sound of that. "On one condition. I'm going to follow you to your building and wait for you. Then I'll follow you ... home."

She nodded. "Thanks. I'd feel a lot better if you did."

Traffic wasn't busy that night, so they pulled right into parking spots in front of the building. Layla got out and blew a kiss to him. How strong she was to be able to function fairly normally in the midst of this and still be so attentive to her father.

What would it be like to have had a father that loved back? Whose mind wasn't destroyed by drugs and alcohol? For the first time in his life, instead of anger, he felt sorry for his father. He'd learned enough about addiction to know it wasn't his father's fault. His father never knew that Jack loved him—despite the beatings, despite the hunger, despite the feeling of not being loved. They'd never shared a single moment of closeness like Clarence and Layla's constant stream of sharing. He checked the time on his phone, then scanned the building.

Where was she?

THIRTY-EIGHT

Layla's heels clicked along the marble floor in the lobby. All the shops on the first level were closed and shuttered. A woman mopped the floor down the hall to the left. Somehow, Layla was comforted by her presence. The elevator door opened immediately, and she stepped in. As it rose, she fought a surge of claustrophobia, trapped in its confines.

You're just being silly. You ride this elevator every day. But it was never this quiet. No annoying elevator music. No juggling her briefcase and purse to make room for all the riders. In the stillness, the *whoosh* of the car rising up to her floor was unsettling, the *ding* announcing her floor jarring.

She stepped out into the corridor, not as brightly lit as during the day but bright enough for the custodian a couple doors down to see how well he was mopping the tile. He had his back to her, and the hood on his sweatshirt was pulled up on his head. She shivered. *Just like the guy who'd kidnapped Dad.* The guy who was stalking her.

Why would Trevor get a job here?

I can find you anywhere you go.

Suddenly, the hair on the back of her neck prickled. The thought of passing the custodian froze her in her tracks.

Don't be silly.

She hurried down the corridor, eyes straight ahead, passing the custodian with a "good evening."

"Good evening, Ms. Forrester." She recognized that voice. He'd spoken at his trial, proclaiming his innocence, and he'd cursed her as he was led away. *I'm not the only one who'll pay.* She almost stumbled. Trevor was here. He could find her anywhere. She turned to look at him.

His eyes gleamed, a smirk on his face. "You're working late tonight. Pretty deserted here."

Her heart hammered as she grasped her keys and practically ran to her office. She unlocked her door and rushed inside. She relocked the door, unable to move away from it, gasping for breath.

Shadows loomed in the dark office lit only by a neon tavern sign across the street, turning the paralegals' desks and book-shelves into ominous shapes. The gauntlet was seared in her brain, so she didn't turn on a light. She crept to her office, careful not to trip on anything that might have been left in the aisle. When she reached her door, the sound of the main door being unlocked sent a *click* echoing in the deserted space.

Oh my God, he's got a key. He was a custodian, of course he had a key. The metallic sound of the mop handle hitting the bucket ricocheted. He was right outside the door. She ducked down next to Angela's desk.

The door swept open and someone entered.

"Layla?"

She let out a sigh and stood up.

"Seth. Thank God you're here."

He turned on a desk light and approached her. "You look like you've seen a ghost."

"Shh. Trevor's out in the hall."

"The custodian?"

"Yes, that's Trevor Hunter, Jimmy's brother."

"So?"

"He's been stalking me. He almost killed Dad."

"I see." He stood in front of her. "You must be very frightened."

She straightened. "Well, he shook me up a bit, but I'm okay."

"Still the ice queen." His eyes glittered in the dim light.

She stepped back. "I'm going to call 911." She pulled out her phone.

He grabbed it, hurling it so it bounced off the nearby desk. "No, you're not."

"What the hell are you doing?"

He stepped toward her, and she backed away.

Black fear drained her at first, the glow of the light behind Seth shimmered, and he swayed in her vision. She wobbled, regretting her choice to wear stilettos all day.

I will not show fear. I will not show fear.

Then white rage shot through her, as though lightning raced along her nerve paths.

"You almost killed my father." Her skin pricked with fury, and she leaned toward him, her hands balled into fists.

"Your old man almost killed me. He got what he deserved. Actually, you got what you deserved. Did I scare you?" His laugh was low and guttural.

She looked toward the door to the hall.

"We're going to stay here until little Trevor is gone, and then you're coming with me."

"No, I'm not." She turned to run, but he grabbed her arm and pulled her back against himself.

"Yes. Yes, you are." His whisper held danger. He cupped her

against him, his arm tightening against her waist, trapping her arms.

"Trev—!" He slapped his hand over her mouth. She wiggled, trying to free herself, but he pulled her in closer.

His mouth was against her ear. "Stop struggling. You can't get away. And little Trevor isn't going to help you."

She couldn't let fear win. She tried biting his hand, but he yanked her head to the side and pinched her nostrils closed with his thumb and index finger. She couldn't breathe. Her heart hammered as panic threatened to consume her. White spots danced before her eyes.

Raising one foot, she jammed her stiletto heel at his knee and scraped it along his shin.

"Ow! Damn you!" He jerked backward, releasing the hand that covered her mouth.

Gulping air, she pivoted, escaping his grip, and bent to remove her shoe.

He reached for her, and she swung her arm with every ounce of rage that pulsed through her, striking him in the temple with the stiletto's heel. The impact of the tip ripping through flesh and striking bone at once sickened and gladdened her.

Seth doubled over, grasping his head. "You bitch." His bellow thundered, echoing in the empty office.

The office door flung open, and Trevor appeared brandishing his mop. "Are you okay, Ms. Forrester?" Quickly taking in the scene, he charged and pinned Seth to a tall file cabinet.

Seth fought against him, but Trevor gave him a struggle.

"Layla!"

She'd never heard a sweeter sound than Jack's voice at that moment.

Jack flew by her toward the struggling men. "Who's the bad guy here?" he called back to her.

"Seth, the older guy."

Seth pushed against the mop that pinned him to the metal cabinet. Trevor pushed back but was losing the battle. Their arms trembled, each emitting rasping grunts as they strained to gain the advantage. Jack rushed to them, helping Trevor hold him down, but Seth fought with the survival instinct of a trapped animal.

Using the cabinet for leverage, he howled as he gave a mighty push, sending Jack and Trevor flying down the aisle. He gripped the broom in both hands and moved on them. Raising it, he struck a blow to Jack's right shoulder.

Jack bellowed but ran full toward him. Trevor circled off to the side, distracting Seth. The two lunged simultaneously, but Seth rammed the mop head into Trevor's gut and spun, smashing the top of the handle across Jack's head. Trevor had doubled over, and Jack was shaking his head, trying to recover.

Layla slipped behind Seth, whipped a metal trash can above her head, and smashed it over his. He collapsed to the floor. Jack and Trevor stood panting and speechless.

Huffing and puffing, Jack bent, hands on his knees. "Thank ... you," he said between breaths.

Trevor gripped his midsection, bending at his waist. "Yes ..." He held up his hand.

"I'll be ... more careful when ... I disagree with you." The corner of Jack's mouth hitched up.

"Good idea." Layla held up her thumb and forefinger and blew at the imaginary gun.

THIRTY-NINE

The red lights flashing through the office windows brought back memories of the day Layla had opened the threatening letter. That day, she'd sat alone in her office waiting for help.

This time she was with people who cared. Jack who held her in his arms, Isaiah, strong and commanding, handcuffing Seth. Even Trevor, who had helped rescue her for reasons she didn't yet understand. And there were two other cops whom she didn't know helping with the arrest.

She turned to Trevor. "Thank you." She shook his hand, then pulled him in for a hug.

He gave a crooked smile. "It was nothing."

"You probably saved my life."

She linked her arm through Jack's. "And thank you. You were like my knight in shining armor."

"That's what PJ said."

She gave him a puzzled look.

As Isaiah was leaving, he paused by her. "You'll need to come down to the station and file a report."

She nodded.

Seth glared at her.

"Well, Seth Thomas, I've cleaned your clock. It's about time you got what you deserved."

Jack groaned, and Trevor look confused.

Isaiah shook his head. "You never cease to amaze me."

The three cops headed out with Seth in tow, but not before he looked back and made a face at her.

AT THE STATION, Layla, Jack, and Trevor sat at Isaiah's desk. Isaiah's fingers flew on the keyboard as they answered his questions. Layla looked around while he typed.

At night the station was pretty quiet without the usual bustle of humanity that flowed through on any given day.

"And why were you there, Mr. Hunter?"

Trevor looked around, then back at Isaiah. "Oh, you mean me? I'm a custodian there. I was working my shift."

Isaiah looked at Layla. She nodded.

"And why were you there, Ms. Forrester?"

Layla blinked at his formality. "I had to pick up my laptop."

"At that time of night?"

She bristled. "Yes."

"Miss Ida wouldn't like that. Especially with a stalker following you around." His expression was deadpan, as serious as if he were questioning a suspect.

Jack choked back a laugh. Trevor, again, looked confused.

Layla lowered her head and glared at him. "And good cops don't release information about their cases. So, Miss Ida need never know about this."

He stared at her. "Miss Ida is formidable."

"On that we agree."

FORTY

Tuesday, May 26

Layla clicked along the gauntlet. All eyes were on her, as usual, but the air trembled with excitement at the news of Seth's arrest. They were dying to know the details. Each said good morning as she passed, today the smiles sincere.

She stopped at the last desk. Fingers froze above keyboards, and the air was electric. "Morning, Paula. Sorry about your trash-can. A new one should arrive this afternoon."

"Thank you, Ms. Forrester. I wondered ..." She let her words fade.

Layla looked around. "Have a good day, everyone." She massaged her throat as if the words had hurt coming out. *That wasn't so hard. I just need practice.*

Stunned paralegals sat in silence for a moment. Finally, one spoke up. "You, too, Ms. Forrester."

Wow. That's better than being flipped off. She hurried past the file cabinet that Trevor had held Seth against the night before. *Maybe we'll replace that cabinet, too.*

"Good morning, Angela."

"What happened last night?" Angela's eyes were wide.

"Come into my office. I'll fill you in." Layla unlocked her office door and ushered in her secretary.

"Angela, I know you were close to Seth ..."

"Look, Ms. Forrester, I'm sorry I slept with him while you two were dating. I didn't know you were together." Her entwined fingers twisted back and forth.

"It's water under the bridge. But if you have feelings for him, you're not going to like what I tell you." Layla tread lightly, careful of Angela's feelings but cautious lest Seth didn't act alone.

"We weren't together long. He was ... difficult."

"Yes. I know." Layla leaned her forearms on her desk. "Seth was my stalker."

Angela eyes widened. "He sent the powder?"

"That and more." Layla described all the threats, ending with what had happened the night before, watching Angela closely. She registered surprise but not disbelief. Angela hadn't known about Seth's plans.

"You mean Seth caused your father's accident? I'm so sorry you've been through all this. No wonder you've been so—that is, you've been under a lot of stress."

"And I'm sorry for any behavior that was rude."

Angela nodded slowly.

"In the past, too, not just this week."

"Got it. Thanks, Ms. Forrester."

"And, Angela, please call me Layla."

Angela nodded and smiled. "Of course ... Layla."

As she left, Mariana entered.

"Hey there. What's new?" her eyes lit up with humor.

"Nothing much."

"So I hear." She rolled her eyes. "C'mon. I want details."

Layla nodded to the outer office. "So do they. How about lunch later? I'll fill you in then."

"Hey, a real invitation? How can I refuse?"

Layla laughed, surprised at how good it felt.

"MORNING, MS. FORRESTER." Jimmy's smile was more mischievous than usual.

"Good morning, Jimmy."

"I have a surprise for you." His grin reached ear to ear.

"Oh? Did Detroit win last night?"

"Better than that. Ta-da." He swung his hands to his right like a game show host. Trevor stepped through the door.

Layla rose to greet him. "Trevor, come in. Jimmy, do you know that Trevor is my hero?"

"Yes, he helped keep you safe last night."

"Yes, he did." She turned to Trevor. "How did you know?"

"He came off the elevator right after you, but he didn't go to the office right away. He waited for you to unlock the door, and then he walked, I don't know, stealthy, like he was up to something. Man, I was right there. I could see him, but I don't think he even noticed me. It was weird and gave me a funny feeling." He rubbed his gut.

"Then I heard somebody yell like they were in pain, so I came in. He never even locked the door behind him. I grabbed my broom and tried to help." He laughed. "At first I didn't know who needed help, you or that guy."

Layla squinted at him. "Trevor, you were pretty angry at me when I prosecuted you. Why did you help me?"

He shrugged and looked at his shoes. He spoke to the floor. "You learn a lot in prison, like what kind of choices you want to make when you get out." He looked at Jimmy. "Jimmy needs me —and I need him. Consider it payback. After all, you took good care of Jimmy while I was in...away." He looked at Layla. "I'm clean now, partly because of you."

Jimmy held out his shirt. "And we got a washing machine, so now my shirt is clean, too!"

Layla embraced the brothers. "Thank you both." Maybe caring about people could change a person's life.

"WHAT THE HELL HAPPENED TO YOU?" Steve Warczynski's voice rang out across the fire station break room.

Jack lightly touched the egg-sized bump at his hairline. *Ouch.* Seth Thomas might not be an athlete, but he had a hell of a swing with that broom.

PJ sauntered over and examined the injury. "Got in another fight with Layla, huh? Listen, if it's not working out for you two, I'd like to step in. She's a great dancer. And hot."

"It's working out just fine for us, PJ, so back off."

"So, what's the deal with your head, man? Did she clock you?" Steve asked.

They sat at the euchre table and, when Nick joined them, Jack described the encounter with Seth Thomas the night before.

"Despite your large, unattractive lump, you're looking pretty chipper this morning." Steve slid the deck of cards out of the box, shuffled, and dealt cards face up until PJ got the first jack.

PJ took the deck and shuffled, squinting at Jack. "You got lucky last night."

Jack pointed at his injury. "Yeah, real lucky."

"But afterward, after filing the police report, you went home with her, didn't you?"

Home. There was that word again. And it sounded so good, so right. Being with Layla was home. He smiled.

PJ slapped the table. "See? I was right. Way to go, man. High five." PJ held up his hand.

Jack ignored it. "Home is exactly where we were."

"Oh, geez. Don't get all mushy on us." PJ lowered his hand.

Steve stared at Jack. "You love her, don't you? This is the real thing." His voice was soft.

Jack nodded. "Yes."

"Great. I'm calling Amber tonight."

"You douche." Jack slugged his arm. "Seriously, I wish you well with her."

Jack studied his hand. All hearts and both red jacks. PJ had turned up the ten of hearts when he dealt. He grinned.

"You can't fool me, Trenton, trying to pretend you have a good hand with that shit-eating grin. You've got nothing"—he glanced at his cards— "and neither have I. Pass."

Both PJ and Nick passed.

Jack stroked his chin as though examining something fascinating. "Hmmm. I guess you'd better pick that up, PJ. And I'll go alone."

"What the—?" Steve slapped his hand face down on the table. "You got me this time, Trenton. I never saw that coming. You didn't have your usual poker face on this time."

Jack led the jack of hearts. "My luck has changed, my friends." He took the trick, then laid down the rest of the cards. The others threw theirs in.

PJ crowed. "Four effing points! Way to finesse Steve, dude." He stood and did a jig around his chair.

The alarm sounded, and they jumped up and ran toward their vehicles.

"Automobile accident at 196 and College," someone yelled.

Jack opened his truck door. His right shoulder didn't ache today.

He considered that a win.

FORTY-ONE

Sunday, May 30

Layla turned her face toward the sun, soaking in its warmth. Today was perfect. Not a cloud in the sky; it was the blue of Jack's eyes. She glanced at him as he cast his line, rod in his right hand, line in his left. *How have I resisted him this long?* She admired the powerful arc of his arm as he cast, swinging the rod back then snapping his wrist, bringing his elbow forward and sweeping out to drop his line in the river.

Dad would love this. And in the near future, he'd be joining them according to the doctors. She breathed deeply of air that promised summer, of freedom from fear, of love that reached down from her toes and spread to the top of her head. She'd heard the term "a heart full of joy," and today she owned it.

Jack fed his line through the eyes of the rod slowly, floating his Blue Wing Olive farther downstream. With the tip of his rod, he followed the progress of the prized fly that Dad had given him. "Guaranteed to draw them in," he'd said when he'd presented it to Jack. Or so Jack had told her. She hadn't been speaking to him at the time.

He glanced back at her, grinning, then turned back to his task just in time to see the fly disappear and the telltale rings disturbing the flow of the stream. He tugged the line and lifted the tip of his rod to set the hook. From the bow of the rod, it looked like a big one.

Layla reeled in her line and hooked her fly on an eye of her rod. While he worked to land the fish, she unclipped the net fastened to the back of his vest. As Jack reeled the fish in, she waded to him, poised to catch the fish that was fighting him like a champ.

"Hold him, Jack! Hold him!" She lowered the net into the water.

Jack fought, struggling to reel in the fish that wriggled and strained against his line. He guided it to the net, and she scooped up the trout. Laying it on the ground, she held the net steady while Jack measured the catch.

"Twenty-two inches!" Jack beamed at her.

She pulled out her cell phone and took his photo holding up his prize.

Jack turned the fish belly up to disorient it enough to stop its squirming before he pulled the hook out of the trout's lip. He turned it over, holding it gently in both hands and lowered it into the water, rocking it back and forth. After a few seconds, the stunned fish juddered into motion, and Jack released it back into the river. The flick of the trout's tail splashed water into Jack's face, and he and Layla laughed.

"I guess that's fair." Jack wiped his face on his sleeve.

"That would have been a delicious dinner," Layla teased.

"I have a better idea for dinner, and it doesn't involve cleaning fish." He placed his hands on her shoulders. "It involves wine and candlelight and you and me."

She smiled into his eyes. "Mmm. Sounds scrumptious. Will food be involved?"

"Eventually." He nuzzled her nose, then along her neck. "If you find it necessary to keep up your strength."

"I might. Too bad you believe in catch and release."

He straightened, his gaze burning into her. "There are some things in life I will never let go of. I will never leave you, Layla. I promise."

"I know." Though she whispered, her belief in him was as solid as the riverbank they stood on. "Sounds like a lifelong commitment to me."

"I wouldn't have it any other way." His dimples sent the usual heat blooming deep within her then coursing through her body.

"I love you, Jack."

"I love you, too, Layla." His kiss was deep, and long, and promised forever.

NOTE TO READERS

Thanks for sharing my characters' journey. Want to know more? Click here and be the first to know about my new books, freebies, and giveaways available only to my followers. Be privy to deleted scenes and upcoming ideas for my new books so you can step into the world of my characters and know them even better. Help me name characters or decide plot direction—you may even see your name in the Acknowledgments!

Want to leave a review of *Exposed*? That would be great! Click here.

Thank you.

Elizabeth

Follow me on:

Website Instagram Twitter BookBub
Author Page Facebook Goodreads

THE CAVANAUGH HOUSE

BOOK 1 IN THE FINGER LAKES MYSTERIES SERIES

June 1968

This might be the biggest mistake I've made yet, thought Jesse Graham.

She climbed out of her three-year-old yellow 1965 Volkswagen Beetle and waded through tall grass and weeds that scratched at her sandal-clad feet. Looming before her, the two-story house—her house—hovered, insinuating more height than it could actually claim. Wrapped in chipped and peeling greenish-yellow paint, the house looked weary, and the once-red front door had faded to a dull russet. The roof sagged, and the tiny porch appeared to be giving up the fight to support the small roof above it. She stared at the house, and the windows stared back, blank. Above the front door, two windows mirrored her dismay as the wood trim above them bowed down. In her twenty-eight years, she had never seen a sadder looking house.

"Oh my God, what have I done?" she breathed.

She closed her green eyes, as startlingly brilliant as her mother's. She suspected they were all she had inherited from the aloof, career-focused woman, for she could see no other similarity.

Once again the fear that she had been the cause of her parents' divorce in her early childhood crept into her mind: did her father leave because of her? Jesse always supposed that her father had wanted a boy, and when she arrived, his disappointment caused him to flee. She shook her head.

"That's nonsense. People don't run away because of the gender of their baby," she said aloud.

She combed her fingers through her thick auburn hair, a gesture she made when concentrating or trying to work through a difficulty. So much sorrow had entered her life recently both on a personal level and a national level with the assassination of Robert Kennedy two weeks earlier and Martin Luther King just months before that. Too much sorrow, and now she faced the consequences of her recent break-up with her fiancé, Robert.

She scanned the yard, which deepened her apprehension. Overgrown bushes hugged the house as if begging it to remain and the lawn had conceded the fight with weeds years before. Now crabgrass, nutsedge and dandelions grew knee-high, hiding even a path to the door. Age-old maple and oak trees dotted the property, providing shade from the June sun, their leaves motionless in the early summer air. The few houses on this road weren't adjacent as they would be in the town, but they were close enough to view this forlorn yard that perched at the dead end of the street. Anything she did would be an improvement.

Jesse's shoulders shook as she began to laugh, silently at first, then shaking with mirth. At first she feared she might be descending into hysteria, but she didn't feel out of control. In fact, she felt very much in control knowing that if she didn't laugh, she would cry. What had she expected? Valet service and a mint on her pillow? The house had been abandoned for over twenty-five years—weeds were going to grow, paint was going to chip. But they were *her* weeds and *her* chipped paint; no one was going to tell her what to do about them. And no one was going to take them away.

Circling the house, she was pleased to see that the windows, with the exception of one that was cracked, were intact, albeit the originals from when the house was built circa 1920. They would not keep summer heat and winter cold at bay.

"No, they're not 'bay' windows," she laughed, then groaned. "Geez, I even make lame jokes when I'm alone."

The house was wider than it was deep, although an addition at the back accommodated a kitchen. Two outbuildings stood farther back on the property, one an outhouse, the other a small carriage house.

"Oh, Lord, I hope there's indoor plumbing."

Plumbing! Not yet; she hadn't contacted the local utility companies to have water or gas and electricity turned on in the house. She checked her watch, relieved to see that it was just 1:30 p.m. She still had time to make it into town and take care of that.

Returning to her car, she rustled through her purse in search of the keys her mother had given her. Her fingers found the horseshoe-shaped key ring, smooth brass worn down by years of use holding three keys: a standard Yale lock key, a smaller brass key and a skeleton key. She headed for the front door and tested the first of three steps leading up to the porch. Feeling confident that they would hold her, she climbed them and faced the door. Her body tingled as if ants crawled beneath her skin; what would she find in there? This was the first step to her new-found independence. No one was coming to her aid if her plans failed. The house was a tumbled-down mess, but wasn't she as well? She had burned many bridges in Rochester, and the bridge with her mother was smoldering. Her father had been out of the picture for years, and she was an only child. Her dear friend Maggie was her sole support system.

Whatever existed on the other side of the door was now a

part of her existence, too. This abandoned and rejected house was all she had. And she was all this house had. *We're in this together.* Straightening her shoulders, she took a deep breath and selected the key. She was surprised that the Yale key worked so easily in the old lock. Her heart pounded as she turned the doorknob and entered the house.

It took a moment for Jesse's eyes to adjust to the dim interior, for the windows were thick with grime, and the trees filtered out most of the sunlight. The centrally located door opened into a small foyer, a room on either side. Straight ahead was a staircase, and beside it, a hall led to the kitchen. Musty air invaded her nostrils, dust turned everything a dull pale gray, and she felt ancient, powdery motes settle upon her like a second skin. Lacy cobwebs stretched from the high corners to the brass light fixtures hanging in the middle of the ceilings. She heard scurrying at the far end of the hall and resisted the urge to run outside.

To her right was the dining room with a door on the far wall that led back to the kitchen. Turning left, she entered the living room, sparsely furnished with drop cloths draped over the pieces. A chair sat perpendicular to a sofa with a round coffee table in front. A floor lamp hung its head in the space between the sofa and chair, and nestled in a far corner was an oak secretary with a drop-down desk. Drooping at the windows were barkcloth drapes that once had boasted white gardenias on a rose background, but now hung in faded tatters, eaten away by dry rot.

Jesse turned slowly, surveying the room.

"Wow," she said. "Wow, wow, wow."

Her thoughts traveled to Robert's apartment with its white leather furniture, glass and chrome accent tables, and carpeting so thick it was like walking on moss. It was as though she was on a "Rat Pack" set when she was there; everything was sleek and modern, tasteful and expensive. She had lived in that world for the past two years. And like its furnishings, that world had turned out to be less ideal than it appeared. A world more than just miles away from this dilapidated house.

Mustering her courage, she pulled the fabric off the sofa. She shrieked as a flurry of grey shapes scattered in all directions—one straight toward her. She panicked as paws scurried across her sandaled foot. Mice! Goosebumps prickled her skin and adrenalin shot though her body. Heart pounding, she ran out the front door, off the porch and bolted to her car. Her knees gave out and she collapsed, trembling.

"Are you okay?"

Grabbing the door handle, she pulled herself up and looked around for the voice's owner.

"I'm over here," he said.

She looked toward the road and saw a blue pickup truck at the end of the driveway. Leaning out the driver's-side window was a man about her age, with tousled red hair. Humor lit up his mouth and softened his strong jawline and rugged face.

"Are you okay?" he repeated as he climbed out of his truck and started toward her.

Jesse brushed herself off and ran her fingers through her hair.

"Oh, yes, I'm fine," she said.

She saw his hazel eyes twinkle with amusement.

"I can see that. In a hurry to get somewhere? I noticed your quick exit."

She looked at her watch and gasped. It was after 2 p.m. If she were going to get any utilities started, she needed to get to town.

"I need to get my utilities started."

Oh, that sounded intelligent. She was a little off balance, and not just because of the mice encounter; this man's gaze was warm and unsettling. He chuckled.

"Well, I would never want to keep a woman from that."

"What I mean is..."

He held out his hand.

"Joe Riley."

She shook his hand and smiled.

"Jesse Graham."

"Nice to meet you, Jessica," he said.

"Not Jessica, just Jesse. The nickname for Jessica is J-E-S-S-I-E. I'm J-E-S-S-E. Pronounced the same, spelled differently."

"Oh, like Jesse James," he said.

"Yeah, I've never heard that one before," she tossed back.

Order your copy of *The Cavanaugh House,* Book One in The Finger Lakes Mysteries with over 600 reviews on Amazon.

ABOUT THE AUTHOR

Believer in dreams-come-true and muses, Elizabeth Meyette is the author of seven books including *The Cavanaugh House, Buried Secrets, The Last Crossing,* and *Love's Courage.* She enjoyed a career in teaching before turning to writing full-time. To quote her friend, "She's not retired, she's re-fired!"

Elizabeth and her husband Rich enjoy living surrounded by the beauty of the Great Lakes. They made an agreement that she cannot cook on writing days after he endured burnt broccoli and overcooked chicken. Fortunately, Rich is an excellent cook.

She credits her muse Boris for keeping the stories coming.

Made in the USA
Monee, IL
09 December 2020